AF499095

Bedroom Eyes

J. J. Pondes

Published by Tales of Flesh Press, 2015.

This is a work of fiction. Similarities to real people, places, or events are entirely coincidental.

BEDROOM EYES

First edition. September 22, 2015.

Copyright © 2015 J. J. Pondes.

ISBN: 979-8201094669

Written by J. J. Pondes.

Bedroom Eyes

by

J J Pondes

Copyright © 2015 J J Pondes

All rights reserved. This book or any portion thereof may not be reproduced or used in any manner whatsoever without the express written permission of the publisher except for the use of brief quotations in a book review.
If any of the sexual situations within this story have occurred in your life consider yourself lucky.

Passenger Pleasure

"All right, girl. See that gorgeous hunk of male ebony standing right over there? He's packing some serious heat," said Nekeisha.

Korah looked up from her reservations terminal and looked at Nekeisha, her coworker. They were both flight stewardesses and were preparing to take in passengers for the newly arrived flight.

At least Korah was working, Nekeisha had her eyes fixed on something other than her own terminal.

"Packing heat?" asked Korah. She looked around at the various passengers waiting to board the plane. They still had a while to wait, yet, but that didn't stop the anal types from getting ready right damn now. "Who is packing heat? Should we inform security?" She tried not to sound worried. This being her very day on the job she did not want to suddenly fly into a panic. Would not do good for appearances.

Nekeisha chuckled. "No, silly girl. Not a gun. A different kind of heat. The kind that is shaped like a salami, is hot and thick, and rewards you for a job well done."

Now Korah was thoroughly perplexed. Was this a first day ribbing she was getting from Nekeisha?

"Okay, I give up. What heat? And who's packing it?" Korah said, a little exasperated.

Nekeisha gave a slight nod at a man standing over at the water fountain by the far wall.

When Korah looked at him she instantly saw what Nekeisha was talking about. The man was wearing loose fitting pants, but it did little to hide the fact he had a rather enormous cock pressed against the fabric of the groin. Even from this distance, with the two girls standing at the gate, it was quite prominent.

Korah gasped a little. It was so huge!

Nekeisha chuckled. "See what I mean? Quite the concealed weapon, don't you think? Maybe we should take him over to the security room and do a nice thorough pat down, just to be sure."

Trying to regain her composure, Korah tried to focus on her terminal. But her eyes were drawn back to the man's package. Wasn't he aware others could see it? Pants or no pants?

Korah shook her head. She actually did not have any real idea what it would look like in the flesh. She was still a virgin, and the frustration was starting to get to her. Sure she'd watched plenty of porn clips, and heard her more experienced friends talk about their sex lives and the naughty things they did, but Korah was actually content to save herself for just the right man.

But who exactly? Someone who had experience, and preferably someone she knew and trusted. And that she wanted to fuck. That was important, too.

"Yeah, wow!" Korah said. "That's... uh... impressive."

"Been a while since I've enjoyed one that size," Nekeisha said. "Makes me all teary eyed."

Korah's eyes were then drawn away from the man's package, and up to his face. Again, she gasped. No. It couldn't be him, could it?

Other passengers crossed in front of the man, obscuring his face. But when they passed Korah finally got a real good look at him.

It was him! It was Antonne!

She was stunned. Antonne was her mother's ex-boyfriend from last year. Korah hadn't spoken to him since he and her mother broke up. Why would they? But, there had been a connection between her and Antonne while he was seeing her mother.

Many times they all hung out together, and Korah felt a strong attraction grow for him. Whether he was aware of it or not, she didn't know. But it was definitely there for Korah. She actually masturbated to him many, many times. Of course, she was unaware of how well endowed he was. But now that she thought of it, her mother did drop subtle hints at how 'fulfilling' Antonne was.

Looking at Antonne's sizable asset, Korah now understood.

And she wanted to be 'fulfilled' by that same big cock, too.

"I know him," Korah said to Nekeisha.

Nekeisha's eyes widened in surprise. "Really? You know that dick?"

"Not the dick. The man attached to that dick." She looked at Nekeisha imploringly. "I have a naughty idea, and I'll need your help to make it happen."

Nekeisha was thunder stuck by this sudden change in her new coworker. She laughed. "Really? Girlfriend, if you have a plan to get that wonderfully big thing inside you while on the job, I'm all for it! People need some spice in their lives after all. Who said flight stewardesses can't either?"

Korah nodded, and took Nekeisha's hand and squeezed it in excitement. "Okay, how long until passengers start to board?"

"About five minutes," Nekeisha said, equally excited at what might happen next.

"Can you cover for me? Do the boarding yourself?" Korah asked.

It wasn't that big of a deal, actually. The flight would be barely a third full if all the reservations actually arrived and boarded.

Nekeisha nodded with enthusiasm. "Yeah, no sweat. But what will you be doing?"

Korah shut down her terminal and grinned. "Why, I have to go pat down that passenger over there. Got to play it safe, right?"

Nekeisha chuckled as Korah walked around the desk and toward Antonne.

He did not notice her approach at first, as he was looking up at one of the television terminals. This profile showed how incredibly sexy he was. Just as Korah remembered him. Her heart beat faster.

As she came up to him, he turned and looked at her. Such a handsome man! Then, there was a moment of confusion, then recognition. His face brightened with delight and Korah's breath caught in her throat.

"Korah? Is that you?" Antonne said with a big smile. He was more than genuinely surprised.

Korah beamed at him. "Sir, may I see your boarding pass please?" She grinned.

At first Antonne was a little confused, but the mischievous look on her face made him chuckle. "Uh, why of course, miss." He handed it to her.

She made a show of looking it over. Then she handed it back, and dropped him a very meaningful wink. "Could you please come with me, sir. We just need to make sure everything is in order."

Now Antonne was confused. "Uh..." he managed to say. His smile started to fade a little.

Korah nodded her head in the direction of the door to the security room. "Much more private in there, sir. To make sure things are all in order." Her eyes widened with meaning.

She could see that it finally clicked with Antonne. He chuckled again, nodded his head in agreement with your little show and said, "Please lead the way, miss."

Calmly she led him across the terminal's waiting area. A glance at the reflection in on of the huge windows showed Antonne looking down at her ass. Catching him in the act made her feel even more thrilled.

Perfect.

At the door she keyed in the combination on the keypad, and opened it. She motioned him inside. "Please go ahead, sir."

Repressing a grin, Antonne went inside. As Korah entered she sneaked a look over her shoulder at Nekeisha. The other stewardess was helping some early bird passengers, but still managed to lock eyes with her. Nekeisha smiled in wonderment.

Korah closed the door, which locked on its own. The room was small and, although it had the official title of security room, it really was just an area for staff to relax and maybe catch a nap between shifts.

Looking curious, Antonne put his jacket and carry on bag on top of the only table.

"Looks very secure," he said, leaning back against the table. His groin was much more prominent at such a close range. The cock bulge was nothing short of extraordinary.

Korah found she was shaking a little. Nerves?

Antonne noticed, and his expression changed to one of concern. "Are you all right, Korah? You look like you're shaking."

Korah found herself closing the short distance between them, and the next moment she was pressed up against him, to both their surprise.

"I'm shaking in anticipation," she said, almost breathless.

Having a beautiful young girl, even one he hasn't seen in a long time, suddenly lathering herself up on his person, didn't seem to phase Antonne in the least. He put his arms around her in a comforting hug. "Anticipation of what?"

"This," Korah said, and kissed him.

His lips met hers without hesitation or protest. As if, he too, had been wanting this for a long time, but could not indulge in the impulse.

They kissed deeply and passionately. Warm, wet, and wanting. Korah found herself rubbing a hand on his cock bulge like it was instinctual for her to do so. His dick was big and thick. And even after a few moments of tongue hockey, it was actually growing in size.

She was immensely pleased to have such an effect on him. She'd desired him ever since he started dating her mother.

But for now, right here, he was all hers!

As she rubbed harder against the thick hidden piece of meat, she found herself moaning into his mouth. Fuck what a turn on this was!

"Now boarding flight 1441 for Las Vegas!" came a sudden voice over the PA system.

Antonne stopped kissing her and said, "That's our flight, isn't it?"

Korah looked coy and dropped to her knees. She started undoing his pants, the bulge bare inches from her nose. "Yup, that is our flight. But we won't be boarding just yet?"

Antonne's eyebrows shot up in mock alarm. "We're not?" He watched as she undid his pants button and started to unzip his fly. "When do we board?"

Korah licked her lips. "We board right after I suck your big fat cock dry." She grinned up at him. "Only way to make sure everything is all secure, sir."

He chuckled. "Yes ma'am!"

With everything undone, Korah yanked his pants down to his knees in one fluid motion. His dick was now straining against his tight underwear, as if begging to be unleashed. Korah was happy to let it out of its confinement.

Gently, she eased his underwear up and over his growing erection, and yanked them down. A big dick swayed out, almost like a falling tree, and bobbed provocatively in front of her face.

It was as immense as it was beautiful. Korah had never seen a real life dick before. Only in pictures and porn clips. And here was the real thing. Big, thick, veiny and standing more at attention by the moment.

His ball sack dangled low, and she found it incredibly arousing to see it jiggle with any minor movement he made.

She arched a brow up at him. "Well, sir," she said. "It appears you have been packing a dangerous weapon upon your person."

Antonne grinned down at her. "It's only dangerous when I use it on flight stewardesses. Is that a crime?"

"Could be. Depends on how you want to use it," Korah said. "Perhaps a closer and more thorough inspection should be done?"

"Be my guest," he said.

Korah grasped the base of his thick shaft. It felt incredibly solid. She gently started to jerk up and down his cock's impressive length. She braced herself against one of his thighs with her other hand.

After a couple of minutes his big dick was standing at full attention. If he wasn't fully erect before he was now. Antonne began to breath heavily.

She jerked harder, tightening her grip slightly, but now she made sure to include his swollen prick with the top of the motion.

"A little too dry?" she asked. She leaned forward and spit on his cock a couple of times getting big gobs of saliva on it. She continued jerking, and the motion felt a little smoother.

Antonne closed his eyes and tilted his head back, completely enjoying being jerked off by this sexy stewardess.

Through the door the could her passengers milling about, oblivious to their little antics. It added a more thrilling charge to what they were doing.

Suddenly, Antonne's eyes opened. He motioned her to stop. His expression was of mild concern.

"Wait," he said. "Are there cameras in here?" He looked around.

Korah giggled. "Hell, no," she said. "People nap in here during shifts." She resumed jerking him off. "If there was I'd be in serious trouble right now."

Antonne chuckled, but moaned as she grasped his nut sack. She gently pulled at it, and rubbed his testicles between her fingers. She could also just see the curve of the bottom part of his butt cheeks as he leaned against the desk. She found the view exhilarating.

"Wonder how this tastes," she said.

"One way to find out," he said.

She slowed her jerking motion and licked the very tip of his swollen prick. Then she kissed the back of its head. She licked again, and again like it was an ice cream cone.

He watched her work eagerly.

She swirled her tongue around his prick, until the purple flesh glistened under the lights.

A few more slow, purposeful kisses turned into her slipping his prick between her puckered lips. She sucked it like a lollipop. From inside her mouth she feathered her tongue over the head.

Now Antonne really moaned loudly.

She decided it was now or never. Slowly, she eased the top portion of his cock deeper into her hot wet mouth. Its girth spread her mouth wide, but she managed it without a problem. She loved how it felt to have his fat cock slide along her tongue and graze the rough of her mouth.

When his prick touched the back of her throat she stopped. Looking down the rest of his length she realized he was only half way inside her.

Now she understood why Nekeisha said she loved big dicks. There was so much to enjoy!

Even slower than before, she eased back up his length, making sure she maintained an intense level of suckage. When her lips slid over his prick, she kissed the tip again.

She gasped slightly, and beamed up at him. A string of spittle extended from the tip of his cock to her bottom lip. "Tastes good," she said.

Antonne nodded, smiling. "So I've been told."

Korah returned her attention to his dick, now wet from her mouth. She slurped up the string of spittle and enveloped his prick again with her lips. Now she started to really suck in earnest.

Moving her head back and forth, she made sure each time she slid his cock into her mouth, more of it went in. From time to time she twisted her grip on his shaft slightly.

The room filled with her wet slurping sucking noise her mouth made with his fat cock inside it.

Soon Antonne started to move his hips with the motion of her head, and she could tell that soon he would cum in her mouth. She was so hungry for it!

"General boarding for passengers 1441 to Las Vegas." Came Nekeisha's voice over the PA system.

Even over the sound of her sucking Antonne's cock, she could tell Nekeisha had a 'hurry up in there' tone to her voice.

Korah switched into overdrive. Sliding her hot wet mouth up and down as much of the length of his dick as she could manage.

Antonne now had a hard grip on the edge of the table. He breathing was fast and heavy.

She knew he was going to pop. Faster and faster she sucked.

"Final boarding call for flight 1441," Nekeisha called. She actually sounded a little worried.

Suddenly, Antonne grabbed the back of Korah's head. "Ah, fuck!" he cried, and started to ram his cock into her throat. Even over her gagging, Korah kept sucking. She'd be damned if she would stop now. He was fucking her throat!

Then, Antonne came. He moaned loudly. From deep within her hot wet mouth Korah felt a hot gush of cum explode from his prick. It shot against the back of her throat.

She kept sucking, only slowing a little bit. She looked up at Antonne who's eyes were closed, and mouth open with pleasure as he spasmed his hips as he shot his full load into her hungry mouth.

Korah felt the pulsating jets of his hot sperm fill her mouth, clog her throat, and slide down it.

Antonne slowed, then stopped. His eyes rolled into the back of his head, and he seemed on the verge of passing out.

Perfect.

When he had shot his very last drop, Korah gave his cock a few quick sucks to get the last of it out of him.

She finally took his fat dick out of her mouth. Cum glazed her lips, and she had a little on her chin. She swallowed loudly.

She licked her lips. “Looks okay to me. I think the danger it presented has past.”

Antonne could only chuckle.

“Final, FINAL boarding call for flight 1441. Would all staff please report to the gate immediately.” Nekeisha was now in full concern mode.

Korah kissed the tip of his prick one last time. “We have to go now sir. Inspection is complete.”

Antonne laughed, but did not have to be told twice.

He eased his wet, cum slick cock into his underwear as he pulled up his pants.

Korah stood. Wiped her chin with her fingers and licked any tasty drops of his cum that remained.

She then straightened her uniform, and went over to the door and opened it.

Antonne grinned at her as he grabbed his carry on bag and jacket.

As he hurried past her she said, “See you on board.”

“I hope so,” he said with a very satisfied smile.

Out in the concourse, they both walked quickly to the gate. Nekeisha was the only one there. No other passengers remained.

Nekeisha checked Antonne through and he quickly moved off down the tunnel to the plane.

Korah came up to Nekeisha, who was beside herself with excitement.

Nekeisha said, “That was cutting it close.”

She cut Korah off when she started to speak. “Tell me later, we have to run, girl!”

They did, running down to the plane and inside. They ignored the annoyed looks they both received from the other flight staff.

Soon, everything was back on schedule and the plane took off.

After being in the air for a while Korah tried to find where Antonne was sitting but couldn't.

"Where the heck did that monster cock get off to?" she asked Nekeisha during a lull between helping passengers settle in. They were resting in the stewardess' nook where they arrange the drink cart.

"He's in my section, at the back near the kitchen," Nekeisha said.

Peeking the curtain and looking out over where the passengers were sitting, Korah found the tasty cum slinger sitting idly in his seat, his row all but empty, reading a magazine.

She found it hard to believe that just a short while ago she was sucking that sexy man dry.

Nekeisha grinned at her. "Well, what the hell happened? You were in there forever. I thought the pilot would send security out looking for you."

Korah smiled, playing coy. "Oh, I was guzzling his cum by the bucket load."

Both girls burst into laughter, but hushed themselves so as to not disturb the nearby passengers.

"And?" Nekeisha asked.

"And what?"

"Anything else happen?"

"I wish. No, there was no time."

"You were sucking down that giant cock the entire time? Impressive."

Korah arched an eyebrow. "Not as impressive as his dick is. My, my, my."

Nekeisha shook her head in awe. "I wish it was me. But I've never had the courage for anything close to being in public."

"Let's switch sections," Korah said.

"Really?" said Nekeisha.

"Do you even have to ask?"

Nekeisha giggled. "My section is your section. And so is he."

Just then, the night time notice bell pleasantly sounded. Both girls went about their business helping passengers settle in for the night. The lights went off in most of the plane except for a few passengers who just couldn't sleep.

Korah noticed that Antonne was still reading. She sauntered over.

He had obviously been waiting for her because he looked up at her approach long before she was standing next to him.

"How are things, sir?"

"Pleasantly secure, thank you," Antonne said, smiling.

Korah chuckled. "Will you be turning in for the night?"

"Not just yet. I'm replaying recent events over in my mind. Can't really sleep. If you know what I mean," he said, looking at her intently.

Korah felt herself getting wet just listening to his voice. The image and feel of his big dick ramming the back of her throat popped in her mind.

"At least let me help you with those pillows, sir," Korah said.

She leaned across him to the empty window seat next to him. She fumbled with a pillow that was in it, but she was making sure her breasts were right in Antonne's face. She put one hand down onto his groin, and gently grabbed his cock. It felt like she got his balls in her grip, too.

Antonne, smiling pretended not to notice and turned his head slightly to give her room. He grunted slightly as she squeezed his package for emphasis.

As she leaned back, again, she released his dick and made sure her full bust grazed across his nose.

"There we go," she said, placing the pillow behind his head. "All better now."

"Thank you, ma'am," he said.

"My pleasure," she said. The words dripped with innuendo. She slowly walked away from him, swaying her hips as suggestively as she could in the limit space of the aisle.

Back in the stewardess nook Korah grabbed Nekeisha with barely repressed excitement.

"I wanna fuck him," she said gleefully.

Nekeisha gave a rueful grin. "Well, duh. That's more than a little obvious, don't you think?"

Korah shook her head. "No, I mean here."

Nekeisha's eyes widened. She'd been doing that a lot over the last few hours. "Here? On the plane?" Nekeisha said.

Korah pulled Nekeisha in close and whispered, "He'll be my first."

"Wow," Nekeisha said. "And such a big cock, too. Lucky girl." She looked concerned. "But where could you do it? Bathrooms are too damn small and you really wouldn't have much time in them."

Korah gave it a good think, too. Then she said. "What about the upper luggage compartment in the back? Is it full up?"

Nekeisha brightened. "Nope! Probably only a quarter full with this flight. Plenty of room to get things done without any unwanted hindrance. And you can lock it from the inside, too. So no one can walk in on you. I think that would be the perfect place!"

Both girls giggled, charged up by the excitement of it all.

"Okay, now I have a plan to get my cherry popped thousands of feet in the air. This is a great job!"

They laughed again.

After a few moments to compose herself, Korah exited the nook and slowly walked down the aisle toward Antonne. She pretended she was looking for any other passengers who might need assistance.

When she got next to him, she glanced around. There weren't any other passengers nearby, other than the ones that were already asleep.

She leaned in close to him.

"Sir, there is an issue with your luggage. Would you come with me please?" she said.

Antonne looked a little confused, but pleased all at the same time. He seemed to instantly get what she was inferring about.

"Yes, of course," he said. "I'd be happy to help you out with this issue."

He stood up from his seat and followed her. Korah slowly led him to the back of the plane past unsuspecting passengers lost in their books or dreams.

Outside of the luggage storage compartment, she did a quick glance around. On the other end of the aisle she saw Nekeisha give her a thumbs up.

The coast was clear.

She opened the compartment door and motioned him inside. She followed him in and closed the door, locking it.

The both stood in a plain featureless section with a pile of luggage neatly stacked at one end.

Korah grinned up at Antonne's bemused expression.

"Alone again," he said.

"Imagine that," she said.

"Are we okay in here? I mean, will any else be joining us?"

Korah giggled. "Nope. Night time pretty sedate, and no other crew will ever come in here."

She moved up against him, and slid her hand down to the bulge in his pants. It was already firming up as she suspected it would. "Let's resume where we left off."

Antonne grinned. "What did you have in mind."

Korah gave him a deep kiss, then said, "I want you to pop my cherry, daddy."

He looked surprised, and smiled widely. "I think that can be managed."

"Good answer," she said. "But we might not have as much time as I would want. I am on the job after all."

Then, with a big grin, she stood back from him and very quickly started to undress.

Antonne laughed, taking the hint. He, too, started to undress.

Soon, both of them were standing naked together in the compartment. They both laughed.

Then they embraced each other and kissed passionately.

Tongues probing and caressing each other's mouths. Their hands exploring the skin and warm flesh of the other.

Antonne squeezed her ample tits as they kissed. He pinched her nipples which made her moan into his mouth. Then he bent down and took on in his mouth, suckling the hard nipple. He flicked it from in his mouth with his tongue.

Korah had grabbed his erect cock and jerked it vigorously. She loved the way its thickness felt in her grip.

Antonne switched tits and began sucking on her other one, getting as much of its supple flesh into his mouth as he could. With a free hand he traced it down her belly, over her thatch of trim pubic hair and onto her waiting moist pussy.

She shuddered slightly.

With one finger, he massaged her clit, gently rubbing it. He reached around with his other hand and grabbed one of her round ass cheeks, pulling her in even closer to him.

Korah enjoyed the sensation of her tit crammed in his suckling mouth, his finger working wonders down against her pussy, and his other hand clutching her ass. What a busy man!

He popped her tit out of his mouth, gave her a deep kiss, then knelt down in front of her. He kissed the top portion of her pussy and she gasped. He kissed it again enjoying its wetness.

Putting his chin deep between her thighs he looked up at her. Then he placed his hot tongue against the very bottom of her pussy so part of it rested on her taint. Then, slowly, he licked upwards. Up over her pussy lips, feeling them splay outwards with the pressure, and again over the top of her clit.

"Wow!" she said.

Then, he did the exact same thing again, face buried between her thighs, tongue all up in her business. He licked upwards again. Then again. And again. Soon his head was moving up and down in a vigorous motion, licking her pussy.

Korah gasped and moaned with each wonderful lick. The wet noise her pussy and his tongue made filled the compartment, even drowning out the sound of the engine vibrations.

Antonne eventually slowed. He kissed her clit once more, then said, "Turn around. Gonna treat myself to your little asshole."

Korah had never even considered such a thing before, but quickly turned around. Her perfectly shaped ass presented itself to Antonne. He smacked both cheeks and enjoyed the jiggle of her young flesh.

Then he grabbed each beautiful ass cheek and pulled them apart, exposing her puckered little anus. He leaned in against her ass, her butt cheeks pressed against the side of his face up to his ears. He gave her asshole a little lick.

She giggled with the sudden sensation.

He licked it again, then again.

Korah instantly knew she absolutely loved having this done to her. Amazing!

He worked her asshole like this for several long moments. Occasionally, he wiggled his face back and forth against her ass cheeks. Then, when she least expected it, he slid a finger into her anus.

"Oh!" she said in surprise.

Antonne probed her asshole, moving his finger in and out over and over. Eventually, he was able to get his entire finger inside her and wiggle it around.

"Oh, daddy!" she hissed. Her naked body shook with the sensation.

He fingered her for several moments, and smacked her ass several times. Then he slowly removed it, stood and turned her around to face him.

They embraced and kissed. To Korah, it was more passionate than before.

"So, you don't have a lot of time, huh?" he asked.

Almost realizing where she actually was, she nodded and pouted. "Yeah, it sucks."

"Then lets get right to the really good stuff, shall we?" he said.

He took Korah by the hand and led her over to a low stack of luggage against the back end of the compartment. He eased her down onto it so she was in a slouched sitting position. Grabbing both her ankles, he spread her legs.

Her glistening ripe pussy almost seemed to beg for his massive cock.

Korah's breath quickened. This was it!

Still holding her ankles, he skillfully guided his dick forward until his swollen prick pressed against the moist folds of her pussy. Then, very gently, he pushed it forward.

Just the tip at first, which made her open her mouth wide, then gasp with pleasure. Soon his cock's head vanished inside her. He eased it out again. Then pushed it back in. Several long moments he worked her tight cunt until he felt she was ready for another inch or two.

After his prick was back inside her fully, he slowly slide a good portion of his shaft inside her as well. Her cunt stretched wide to engulf his thick rod.

Korah was beside herself was both pleasure and pain. "Ah, fuck me!" she said.

Antonne pushed more of his fat cock inside. Then eased it out again, then in. He started to do this a little faster, and after several pelvic thrusts he would push more of his length deeper inside her.

Soon, he was in full form, fucking her hard. Cock sliding all the way in and out to the point where his prick was exposed, then he slid it all in again.

Korah could no longer form words, her eyes rolled into the back of her head. She was squeezing both her tits hard and pinching their nipples. She grunted at the feel of his thick shaft stretching her tight pussy wide.

Soon he shifted has hands from her ankles to the the luggage beneath her shoulders and began to pump up and down with full force. Like a pile driver he slammed her tight virgin pussy over and over and over again.

Korah came. It welled up from deep within her, then rushed over her body like a blooming flower. She half moaned, half screamed with her orgasm. Still, Antonne did not let up, pounding her relentlessly.

Her cunt gushed with her orgasm, pussy juice shooting everywhere it could with a giant cock ramming into it.

Her sweaty naked young body bucked and heaved. She felt light headed as if she was about to pass out.

Antonne slowed a little, then slipped out of her hot wet cunt.

His fat cock was slick with her pussy juice, and there was even a little bit of blood from her pierced maidenhead. He stroked it hard and fast.

"Come here and open your mouth!" he panted.

Korah came to her senses. "Yes, daddy! Fill me with that cum of yours!" She leaned forward and took his fat prick into her mouth.

As he stroked his long thick shaft, she sucked on its head.

Then, Antonne exploded into her mouth (again!). Hot jets of sticky cum gushed into her mouth, and down her throat.

He bucked and moaned with his orgasm, and Korah kept his prick firmly locked between her lips, sucking down ever last warm drop of him.

Finally, Antonne collapsed onto her, and the held each other in a warm, sweaty and very satisfied embrace.

The motion of the plane's vibrations, and their post-fuck fatigue threatened to send them both to sleep.

"I have to go back to work, daddy." Korah said, pouting but happy at the same time."

"Okay," he said.

They kissed, then quickly dressed.

Once fully clothed, they gave each other a once over to make sure everything looked okay.

Korah grinned. "Do we look like two people who just fucked their brains out in the back of the plane at thirty thousand feet?"

Antonne laughed. "I hope so."

She opened the door and checked to make sure the coast was clear. Then motioned him to go back to his seat.

As he passed her, she gave him a swift pat on the ass and said, "I hope you had a pleasant flight!"

END

Big Man

"With a booty like yours, you are going to be the most popular girl with all the men here in the office," Breyann said.

Latoya nearly dropped the stack of folders she had cradled in her arms when she heard this. "Breyann!" she said. "What if someone hears you say that?" Latoya looked around the massive filing room they were in, but no one else was around.

Breyann was a great friend of Latoya's, even got her started in a new job at the huge corporation she works at. But at times, she could say the most bizarre things.

"What?" Breyann said, looking coy. "It's true. The men here will fall all over themselves to get at your lovely behind. Hell, I bet some of the women would, too."

Latoya just rolled her eyes at her friend. For her first week on the job, things had been more or less stressful, learning how everything works. Of course, it really didn't help when Breyann was blurting out things like that at the strangest times. Made Latoya blush on more than one occasion.

Latoya shook her head, "I'm willing to do what it takes to get ahead and climb the corporate ladder, but wiggling my booty won't get me far at all."

Breyann grinned. "Well, if I had a body like yours, I'd use it to its full advantage and sleep my way to the top. I mean, if you don't you could be stuck in this room filing for the rest of your life." She motioned at all the filing cabinets and teetering stacks of folders waiting for a home. And it was Latoya's job to find it.

Even without a college education, which she could never afford anyways, Latoya had done fairly well for herself. But she could never truly get ahead and move upwards in a company.

And she had the most rotten luck. Her last company shut down suddenly, tossing her into the streets. She begged Breyann for a job, any job, and managed to get this one. Grand and impressive as it was: Filing Clerk.

Breyann saw Latoya thinking pensively. She leaned over. "And if you offered that sweet cherry of yours to one of the upper management, I can absolutely guarantee you'd be promoted to, like, Queen of Human Resources, or some bullshit like that." She laughed.

Latoya chuckled. There was something to what Breyann said. What hope did she have anyway? Maybe flirting with some of the managers could get her even a secretaries position, at least. Better than in this dungeon.

And as for her virginity? She was saving that for someone really special.

Suddenly Kimberly, their supervisor, poked her head in the door. "Girls. I need you to stop doing that for now. You are both needed in the Upper Office to do some work there. I just got the call and they need you both right away."

Breyann looked shocked. "Us? Really?"

Kimberly shrugged. "They asked me for two filing clerks. So that makes it you two. Hurry on up now."

Latoya and Breyann stood, placing their folders on other piles. "Which office in particular?" Breyann asked as she brushed off her skirt.

"Mr. Brown's," Kimberly said, then turned and left.

Breyann led Latoya to the elevators. As they waited Latoya said, "You know, I don't even know the names of the big head honchos here, yet. Which one is Brown?"

The doors opened and the went inside. Breyann punched the button for the top floor. "Brown is Dameon Brown. As in, the founder of this place, and more or less the owner."

Latoya scrunched her face up. "Odd. That name rings a bell."

Breyann shrugged. She was using the elevators wall mirrors to adjust her breasts. "It should. The guy's been in Forbes enough time they should change the name of the magazine to his. People in the office call him Big Man. And not just cause he's rich." She giggled.

Latoya shook her head. "No, that's not it." She couldn't put her finger on it and it bugged her.

Breyann looked over at Latoya. "Oh, damn girl! You got it, and this is the place to flaunt it." She reached over and plucked open a button on Latoya's blouse exposing a sensual hint of cleavage. "So flaunt it!"

Before Latoya could reach up and do up the button the elevator doors suddenly slid open.

The office they entered was nothing short of immaculate and stunning. It glowed wealth from every surface. The best of everything was used in this place.

Latoya was wide eyed as she followed Breyann. Here she had just been in the office dungeon and now she was in heaven.

I could get used to working up here, she thought.

They stopped outside a beautiful set of oak double doors that were partially opened. Breyann patted Latoya's ass. "Show time girl," she said. Breyann knocked as she and Latoya scooted inside.

A frustrated middle aged woman was hustling around behind a desk. She smiled at Breyann and Latoya as they entered.

"Did Kimberly send you up?"

"Yes, Shawna." Breyann said.

"Good," Shawna said. "A whole bunch of boxes came from the warehouse and need to be filed right away. They're in the next room over. Could you please start on them right away?"

"Of, course," Breyann said and started toward the opposite doorway.

Just then, the door to another inner office opened. Latoya sensed this was the President's office, and Shawna was his secretary.

A stunningly handsome man stepped out. He was wearing an expensive suit and looked like he just stepped out of a men's fashion show.

Latoya gasped. *She knew him!*

"Shawna, could you please get me those..." he stopped in mid-sentence, taken aback by Latoya's presence.

"Latoya?" the President said, obviously shocked.

"Dameon!" Latoya said, beaming happily. *Oh, my, oh, my.*

It was him! Her Dameon!

Shawna and Breyann looked equally perplexed. "You know each other?" Shawna asked.

Dameon chuckled, went over to Latoya and gave her a quick hug. Latoya hugged back, eagerly.

God he felt good!

Dameon seemed to get over his shock and said. "Why yes. I knew her from, what was it? Two years back." He grinned at Latoya. "I dated her mother for a time."

Latoya felt a blush coming. Dameon not only dated her mom for a while, he made it a nightly ritual to fuck the hell out of her, too. Latoya could hear them going at it and it actually made her jealous.

He's the one! He's the one I want to be my first!

Shawna and Breyann stared in Latoya in confused amazement.

"Small world," Breyann said, with just the hint of a mischievous smile.

Dameon asked Latoya, "So you're with us then? That's great."

Oh, I'm with you all right, Latoya thought. *I'm with you all the way right up until you cum inside my freshly fucked virgin cunt!*

Latoya blanched at the sudden, and very dirty thought. What had gotten into her?

Dameon gave Latoya's shoulder a slight squeeze. "Good to see you again, Latoya. We'll talk later." He turned to continue talking to Shawna about business, and Breyann pulled Latoya away and into the side filing office.

It was like their own filing room downstairs, only much nicer. It was like heaven, but for file folders.

Breyann's eyes were wide with conspiracy. "Holy shit, girlfriend." She slapped Latoya's arm. "You didn't tell me you were tight with the big man!"

Latoya was stilled surprised. "I didn't know this was his company."

"And did you see the way he looked at you?" Breyann said with a wide grin. "It was like you were something edible. You sure it was your mother he wanted to screw all the time?"

Latoya laughed and shook her head, not answering.

As they started filing Latoya's mind was racing. Dameon hung around her house a lot, now that she thought about it. And on more than one occasion Latoya and Dameon had given each other looks. Meaningful looks that indicated if her mother wasn't present, something very special could have happened between them.

Then there was that one time Dameon had stepped out of the shower, just wearing a towel, and ran into Latoya. They had smiled at each other then, too. Only it felt different. When Dameon had gone into her mother's bedroom, Latoya had wanted it to be her own room he was going into.

And now she worked for him. And he was very happy to see her.

She grinned at the possibilities.

Just then there was a commotion in the inner office. Breyann and Latoya went over to find Shawna anxious and upset.

Dameon had come in from his office as well. "What's wrong, Shawna?" he asked.

"My basement just flooded! I have to get home right away." Shawna fumbled about, grabbing her purse and coat. "I'll get human resources to send someone up from the secretary pool to fill in for me."

Dameon held up his hands. "Don't worry about that. Just get home and take care of things."

Shawna rushed out of the office. Breyann and Latoya were returning to the filing room when Dameon said, "Latoya. Would you mind sitting in for Shawna for the rest of the day?"

Breyann gave an obvious sidelong meaningful glance to Latoya, which Latoya ignored.

"Yes, Dameon. I would be happy to do that for you," Latoya said.

Dameon grinned and went back into his office, closing the door.

Latoya slapped Breyann's arm. "Into the filing room with you, filing wench!"

Before she went inside Breyann leaned over and said, "Time to work on getting that promotion!" Then vanished.

Latoya sat at Shawna's desk, which was very clean and orderly. She had down some secretarial work before, so this was nothing new. But to do it for the man she now knew was the one she wanted to give herself to? That made it all the more pleasurable.

After about twenty minutes of boredom, and thinking about how to snag Dameon for herself, she decided to take the initiative. She knew Dameon. Was aware, from his time with her mother, that he was quite the sex fiend. Now she wanted him to be her sex fiend.

She worked up the courage and lightly knocked on his door.

"Come in!" he called.

Latoya slipped inside his office and quietly closed the door behind him. His office was stunning as it was huge. His desk was immense.

She looked up from it to Dameon and found him smiling at her. And not just any smile either. The kind of smile he used to give her mother.

"Latoya," he said. "Very happy to see that you are working for me now."

Was that innuendo in his voice? She hoped so.

Latoya glided into the room, and drifted toward his desk. He had a gravity that pulled her along.

"I was hoping we could have that chat now," Latoya said, running her finger along the end of his desk, walking closer to him.

Dameon's smile grew bigger. "Of course, what did you have in mind?"

Latoya sauntered behind his big plush chair where he couldn't see her. She quickly undid a button on her blouse. "Oh," she said, unbuttoning another. "I think we should take some time to get to know each other better. Since we'll be working together. I'd like that." She ran a finger across the back of his shoulders, broad and strong.

And rich.

"I'd like that. But I have to be honest, I have a quick meeting in about..." Dameon didn't get to finish as Latoya came around the other side of his chair. Her blouse was wide open, both perky tits exposed and pointed at Dameon's shocked expression.

Latoya leaned over him so her breasts were almost in his face. "We have a meeting, Dameon. And it won't be quick." Without waiting for an invite, Latoya gently grabbed the back of Dameon's head and pulled against one of her breasts.

Dameon needed no encouragement. He willingly had his face pressed against her tit, and instantly inhaled a nipple, and most of her breast, into his hot mouth.

Latoya gasped, enjoying the feel of his face against her bare skin. She knew her magnificent tits would be an asset around here.

Dameon sucked hard, while hungrily flicking her hard nipple with his tongue. As he did so, Latoya eased her other hand into his lap. Underneath the expensive fabric of his pants, his cock was swelling quickly.

Perfect.

When she was certain he wouldn't stop, she took his head with both hands and eased it back. Her tit popped out of his mouth causing him to gasp.

She kissed him, deep and passionately. Hot tongues intertwined, sucking on each others wet lips. The kissed like this for several long moments, then she gently pulled his head back and grinned.

"You missed one," Latoya said.

Genuinely confused, but in a cute way, Dameon said, "Missed one? One wha..."

She shoved his face against her other boob. He eagerly attached his mouth to her nipple, gently biting and teething it. He reached up and squeezed her other breast hard, pinching its nipple.

Latoya did a hand check on his hidden cock, and sure enough it was like a steel rod hidden away. She rubbed at it. Dameon sucked at her tit harder, switching between them now. Biting, licking, sucking and teething them, all the while grabbing and squeezing them both.

She then pulled him away again, kissing him deeply.

She then hoped up to sit on his desk. With one foot she pressed it against his groin. Dameon watched her eagerly, waiting to see what she wanted to do next.

"Want to know a secret?" she said.

"What?" Dameon said.

"I'm not wearing any panties," she declared. And with that, she cinched up her skirt past her hips.

And sure enough, she wasn't wearing anything at all under there.

Her well shaved pussy glistened wetly as she spread her legs wide, knees up in the air. "Lick me," she commanded.

Dameon pulled his chair closer to the desk and clasped her legs around the thighs with his hands. He gently kissed her exposed clit and Latoya moaned. She leaned back on her elbows on top of his desk, and played with her tits.

Dameon began to lick her wet pussy with earnest. Sticking his tongue down almost between her butt cheeks, the tip grazing her little asshole, then slowly sliding it up over her moist soft pussy lips, then over her clitoral hood.

He licked her like that again, and again. Latoya moaned louder, putting a hand behind his head to keep his face buried between her spread thighs.

Dameon then sucked at her clit, keeping his mouth over it. His tongue flickered at it and working wonders. Latoya twitched occasionally from the intensity of the feeling of his hot wet tongue smothering her clit. He wiggle his head back and forth, clit firmly locked between his lips, tongue flickering against it.

Latoya shivered and groaned. It was amazing and wonderful to have her pussy eaten out. And Dameon was so good at it!

Bet mom doesn't taste as good as me! She thought, wickedly.

Slurping and sucking, he licked every portion of her pussy. He spread her lips, exposing the beautiful pink inside. He gently probed the inside with his tongue, his nose pressed against her trim thatch of pubic hair.

Wiggling his tongue inside her hot wetness, he reached up and cupped one of her tits, squeezing it. He pinched its nipple. Her pussy lips were clasped onto his cheeks, his chin firmly jammed between her ass cheeks pressing up against her little asshole.

He moaned into her wetness. She moaned, too.

As he suckled her clit, she sat up, and grinned at him. "You're so damn good at that!"

He grinned around her pussy. "Lots of practise," he said. He resumed eating her out.

Lots of practise on my mom? She thought. *Well, he's got it better now! Maybe I should turn the tables on him.*

Legs still spread wide, she reached forward and took his head in her hands again. Gently, he pushed him away from her.

Dameon looked hurt from be denied this hot wet meal, but managed to lick her pussy one more time before she had pushed him back into a sitting position. She then stood in front of him and he kissed her belly, reached around and smacked her ass.

She then knelt in front of him. Dameon leaned back, with his legs open wide in front of him.

"Let's see what we got here," Latoya said.

And see what mom got to enjoy all those times!

She fumbled with his belt, undoing it. Then she unzipped his fly. He looked down on her with a smile of anticipation. Latoya pulled his pants down almost to his knees.

His fat cock popped out at her from beneath the bottom of his shirt. She grabbed at it eagerly.

"Well, well," she said, admiring it. "You been hiding this from me this whole time, mister?"

Dameon pulled his shirt up so to give her a better view. "It's all your's now," he said, smiling.

She leaned forward, his fat cock in her grasp, mouth open only inches away from taking it into her, when there was a sudden knock at the door!

"Oh, shit," Dameon hissed. "My meeting."

Both of them froze not knowing quite what to do. Someone fumbled with the doorknob. "Dameon, are you in?" came a voice from the other side of the door.

Latoya then made a quick decision, the only one to keep them from being caught. She scooted back under the desk, which was fully enclosed, and pulled Dameon forward with her my his fat erect cock.

Dameon, obviously at a loss to how to handle the situation, let her pull him in with her. From the waist up he would look fully clothed.

Just then the door to the office opened. "Dameon! There you are. Shawna isn't there so I let myself in. I hope that's alright."

"Not at all Trevor," Dameon sounded calm, but a little tense. Hard not to when you have a half naked hottie under your desk holding your erection.

The two men started talking business, and after a few moments Latoya knew she had not been detected. She looked around. She could not be seen from the other side of the desk since it went down to floor and was pressed firmly into the carpeting.

Fear morphed into a thrill. Dameon's cock was still hard in her grip. And from this angle she could see his hanging ball sack better. His testicles seemed to call for her.

She leaned forward, her head already between his knees under the desk, and pushed in closer to his nuts. They were large and hefty.

And very suckable.

She licked at his sack while still griping his dick. Playing with each one with her tongue. The texture was odd to her, but very pleasant.

Latoya then sucked one of his balls in between her lips.

Dameon was speaking at that very moment and there was a definite hitch to his speech, but he recovered and kept talking. She had the sense he was trying to wrap things up quickly, but she didn't really want that. This was fun.

She sucked the testicle all the way into her mouth, as far as his scrotum sack would allow. She caressed it in her hot wet mouth with her tongue feeling it slide about in its limited space.

Slowly, she eased her head back and while still sucking quietly, let it pop out of her mouth. It dangled wetly. She then turned her attention to the other one. It was a little smaller than the first, but still filled her mouth when she slowly sucked it in.

Again, she caressed it with her tongue, sucking slowly and softly. She stroked his erect cock up and down, careful not to go to fast, or accidentally pull at his shirt. Her nose was pressed up against the base of his shaft.

The feeling and imagery of this made her pussy ache to be violated, and soon.

The men kept talking, but Latoya didn't really pay that much attention. Happy down under here to explore his cock and balls.

She let the ball pop out of her mouth, and this time she started to lick at his cock's base. Slowly, methodically, she licked up his length. There was enough room under her that she could fit her head up over the end of his cock.

When she reached his swollen prick, she gently kissed it all over, flickering it occasionally with her tongue. Once it was wet from her attention, she placed its head into her hot mouth.

Again, Dameon happened to be speaking, and again there was a hitch in his voice. He kept talking like there was nothing wrong. Like there wasn't a hot bitch under his desk with his cock in her mouth.

Latoya started to suck. Very slowly, very quietly. Almost glacial in movement, but she knew Dameon was finding it intense. She grinned around the girth of his cock.

Down his shaft, then up. Her lips were firmly fixed around his cock, getting it nice and wet with her spit. She kept at this, since she really didn't have anything else to do down here to pass the time. So she sucked his fat cock.

She was careful not to make any noise, but her suction on his dick was full on. Up and down, up and down she moved her head, his hot dick sliding in her hot mouth.

When she reached his prick she swirled her tongue around it, then lunged downward, taking his entire length into her in one movement. She felt his prick press against the back of her throat. She held it there.

Dameon's body quivered slightly.

With his full length of his cock firmly lodged in her head, she heard him tell the other man that maybe they could finish this up tomorrow.

The other man agreed and left.

"Please close the door behind you," Dameon said.

She heard the door close.

Dameon then leaned back, eyes wide with amazement as he looked down at her.

As he moved back, his cock unsheathed itself from her throat and mouth, causing her to cough.

"My, God girl! You are a naughty one, aren't you?" He said grinning.

Mouth and chin covered in spit, Latoya grinned back. "Naughty with you is all I want to know, daddy."

Dameon chuckled.

Latoya then stood. "I want you, daddy," she said. She kissed him. "I want you inside me. Pop my cherry, daddy!"

Dameon kissed her back. He was still a little flustered from almost being caught, and then having his balls and dick sucked for the last twenty minutes.

"Yes!" Dameon gasped.

He turned the younger woman around and bent her over his desk. He smacked her ass with delight and Latoya yelped with pleasure.

Dameon's big fat cock was slick with Latoya's spit, and he very slowly eased his prick between the moist soft lips of her pussy. Then he paused, gripping a butt cheek in each hand.

"Are you ready for this, naughty little girl?" he asked. He knew what the answer would be.

"Yes!" Latoya gasped. "Fuck me, daddy! Fuck me!"

Slowly, he pushed his cock forward into her. First his swollen prick vanished into her hot wetness. She was tight. Real tight. He eased out a bit, then pushed in again, this time a tiny bit more of his big dick.

He did this several times, taking care not to plow her right away. He'd get to that soon enough.

Eventually, not only dick his prick vanish into her, but the first two inches of his shaft. Latoya groaned. He eased out and in, out and in. Her little asshole was looking up at him, so he rubbed at it with a thumb. All the while he worked himself further into her hot wet flesh.

Soon, he was pushed almost his entire length into her. Latoya was grunting and moaning now, just like he thought she would.

He could see her tight pussy was stretched out encompass his wide girth. Her pussy lips clasping around him completely.

Faster he started to move, his pelvic thrusts becoming more and more frantic.

She was tight, and Latoya knew she was tight. The pleasure and the pain enveloped her. And she loved it! It felt good to be fucked!

"Harder!" she managed to say between gasps.

Dameon chuckled and smacked her ass hard. "You sure? You've been naughty?"

"Yes, daddy! I've been naughty. Fuck me harder!"

"Well, okay then!" Dameon said and increased the power in his thrusts. He was smacking against her hard, her ass cheeks jiggling quickly with each hit. He was really tapping that lovely ass.

On and on he fucked her. He reached down and around to squeeze her tits, all the while pounding away. She looked amazing. She felt amazing.

Latoya was moaning loudly now. Unable to contain herself, lost in the feeling of being fucked so hard.

"Oh, God!" Dameon cried. He was going to cum.

Latoya slide him out of her and quickly spun around. Dameon was stroking his big dick, ready to explode.

Latoya got onto her knees and opened her mouth wide, big beautiful eyes looking up at him hungrily.

Dameon popped. He came all over her face. Across her forehead, down her nose and even into a nostril. Over her cheeks, and he even manage to get some into her hair.

He gasped, and his squirting subsided.

Latoya quickly took his cock into her mouth. A few squirts of cum spilt over her tongue and against the back of her throat. She could taste her pussy on his cock, and she loved it.

She sucked at his dick, getting the last of his hot seed, and swallowing it. Cum dribbled from the corners of her mouth and down her chin. Some even got on her tits.

Dameon looked down at her, grinning widely.

"Latoya, my naughty little girl. You just got yourself a promotion!"

END

For His Pleasure

Hakim loved books almost as much as he loved sex. Almost.

Yet, he never thought the two would actually collide together until he met the cute new employee at the book store.

He had been going to that store for many years. Occasionally, there would be an attractive clerk working there. Usually, it was someone who primarily stocked shelves with all the new releases. The work itself required lots of kneeling, stretching and bending.

When one of these cuties worked in his area, he found that sitting in one of the lounge chairs gave him a good view of their comings and goings.

Sadly, though, there seemed to be a high turnaround at the store. Whether to internal staff politics, general attrition (he couldn't imagine doing that type of work for years) or they here migrated to other branches, he never knew. But many hot, and/or cute, (or both) shelf stockers simply vanished from his almost weekly appreciations.

Or maybe they left because of him? He'd often wondered how obvious he was when he sneaked glances at their bums as the sauntered past, or bent down to add some books (That was certainly his favourite part of their job!). Also, as they were lost in the mundane concentration of their work, the almost never realized he was staring at their breasts. Side boob view was another favourite. You may not get a full appreciation of breasts full on, masked by a sweater or baggy blouse. But turned to the side, the breast was particularly arousing.

Then one day, there was a new little cute librarian. She was young, short in stature, with a very curvy figure. Thankfully, a lot of her books needed stocking right in front of where he was sitting.

Playing casual, he peeked at her from over the edge of his book, thus allowing him to ogle her magnificent butt. *Jeans were created to be worn by this girl*, he thought.

She had bent over, revealing the beautiful round shape of her ass.

He felt himself getting hard, and he looked down at his crotch, making sure everything was still in order and not bulging out at a revealing angle.

"Found what you are looking for?" asked a pleasant female voice.

He looked up, and blanched. It was her. The curvy cutie was standing directly in front of him.

What did she mean? Looking for my boner? A book? Her?

"Uh," was all he could manage in that moment of shock. He became frighteningly aware of bulge growing bigger.

Did her eyes just flicker down at it? He thought, embarrassed. Maybe was she just looking at the book in his hand?

"Enjoying the selection?" she asked, with a crook of her eyebrow. Her expression seemed to show more than a passing interest in what his answer could be.

Was she flirting with him?

"Yeah, great selection. Thanks," he said. *Geez, could I sound more stupid?*

"I'm Malaya," she suddenly offered. "Just started here today."

He was a little tongue tied, not expecting to have to actually *interact* with this object of desire. *Who'd of thunk of such a concept?*

"Hakim," he stammered. His heart was now thundering against his chest. Hopefully, his face didn't go red like it usually did when he was flustered.

"Well, Hakim," she said with a smile and a wink. "Maybe I'll see you around?"

"Yeah, definitely," he said.

She turned to go, but paused. His heart stopped.

She nodded her head at his... crotch? At his growing hard on? He wanted to cross his legs but his erection would just make it look even funnier.

"By the way, you're reading it upside down," she grinned wickedly at him, and walked away, pushing the cart. He could have sworn she put in an extra bit of sway to those perfect hips.

He watched her leave, a bit in a daze. Looking at the book in his hands, he saw that she was right.

Stunned, he waited for his hard on to die down. He even managed to read a little of the book (right side up this Hakime), until he felt he had embarrassed himself enough for one day.

He was walking towards the exit when he suddenly heard something.

"Hakim!" someone hissed from behind. He turned and was struck dumb when he saw that it was Malaya. She was leaning around the end of a bookshelf, out of sight of the front door cash register. She peeked down toward the cashier then, looking back at him, waved his hand at him, indicating he should come over.

Thankfully, his legs took the initiative and propelled him to her, before his brain could screw things up.

When he got close, and obviously wasn't moving fast enough for her, she grabbed his arm and pulled him behind the shelves. Her firm touch electrified his bare skin. He found himself grinning.

She grinned back. "Got a question for you, Hakim." she said, looking quite beautiful.

"Okay," was all he could say.

"Wanna fuck my brains out?"

His breath caught.

Oh.

My.

God.

His brain had seized up. Miraculously, he found himself nodding.

Pleased, she took his hand and quickly led him into a back storage room, which was filled with books, and boxes, from top to bottom. She closed the door behind them.

"Now, you're going to have to wait her until closing and everyone else leaves." She looked up at him with big wide stunning eyes that melted his heart and began to stiffen his crotch again. "Will you wait here for me, Hakim?"

Duh.

Shrugging, he said, "Yeah, no problem, he said, casually. Like getting propositioned by store clerks was an everyday occurrence for him.

She nodded, but looked at him as if analyzing his honesty. "You know what?" she said.

"What?"

"Let me give you a little taste of what you can expect if you do stay."

Before he could say anything she dropped to her knees in front of him. His eyes widened, and his boner screamed to be released.

"Whip it out," she said.

There is a God! his brain seemed to cheer at him.

"Hurry," she said. "I'm only suppose to be on my coffee break." She looked up at him. "And I wanna little taste, too."

He had never unbuckled his belt, and undid his zipper, that fast before in his life. His erect dick practically popped out at her with the sudden motion of pulling down his pants past his waist.

She giggled a little, but immediately grabbed it. The warmth of her hand on his throbbing member, nearly made him cum right there, but he grit his teeth.

"Mmmm," she said. She very gently kissed the tip of his dick. "I like the taste of that." She stuck out her tongue and flickered it against his prick. She did this for several moments, alternating between kissing and flickering at it.

Then, suddenly, she opened her mouth wide and lunged forward. Nearly his entire cock was swallowed in one motion. He felt the top of his dick slide against the roof of her mouth, and lodge in the back of her hot throat.

He moaned.

"Mmmm," she said again. At least that's what it sounded like. She did have a big cock in her mouth, after all.

Clinching her lips around his girth, she began to move her head up and down. She sucked at him, gently.

Soon, the only thing he could feel was her determined grip at the base of his shaft and part of her palm against his balls, and the hot sensation of the wonderful wet friction of his member sliding in and out of her mouth.

He moaned again. He was now having a heck of a time not cumming and preventing hot jizz from exploding out of the back of her head.

"Malaya to the front cash! Malaya to the front cash!" suddenly said a loud voice.

They both froze.

It was the intercom.

But she didn't lose her cool. Slowly, almost deliberately, she slide up his shaft, which now was slick with her spittle. Her sucking lips slide over his prick, but remained locked on the very tip of it. As she looked up at him he felt her tongue flicker feather-like at the tip.

Then she pulled it out and gave it one last quick kiss. She stood, and he found himself standing in front of her holding his wet throbbing dick. *Was it over?*

"This is not over," she said, as if reading his thoughts. She stood on her tip toes and kissed him on the lips.

"I liked that taste, and I'll be back for more," she said. "Think you can wait for me?" She grinned evilly.

"Yeah!" he gasped. *Sweet Lord Almighty, Yes!*

And with that, she slipped out the door, and closed it behind her, locking it.

He was left standing there, pants down to his knees, holding his dick.

Not wanting to rub one out (gotta save that for later), he did up his pants, and spent the Hakime reading while waiting.

It didn't take long. Soon, some of the lights went off, but a bank of them stayed on in the storage room. Closing time.

Then, after what seemed like forever, the door clicked open, and for a brief moment, he thought someone other than Malaya was going to come in and find him there.

It wasn't. Face beaming, Malaya entered, and relocked the door behind her.

"Well, well, well," she said. "Tired of waiting?"

He sprang to his feet from the chair he had been reading in. "Nope, not at all. Uh, are we alone now?"

She smiled. "Yes, and let me prove it." Suddenly, in one fluid motion, she pulled off her shirt. Hakim was rendered speechless, as she was not wearing a bra (which he had suspected), and her small, perky breasts presented themselves to the world to be admired.

He also couldn't help but notice she had a flat, well defined tummy.

"Wow," he said.

"It gets better," with a couple of quick motions, she pulled down her jeans, as well as her thong panties, down to her ankles. She grinned at him as she kicked off her shoes, and stepped out of everything.

Eager to join in the festivities, Hakim quickly pulled off his own shirt, and tossed it. Then he started on his pants, before she walked over to him, and put her hands on his belt buckle. His eyes were on the trim triangle of hair that was between her well muscled thighs.

"Wait, not yet," she said.

Certain he would do as she asked, she wiggled over to the desk. Hakim's eyes were locked on that amazingly big firm butt, and the tiny peek of a pussy they presented.

She glanced back at him, then bent straight over the desk, so her elbows were leaning on the top. Wiggling her ass, Hakim could now see the well shaved pinkness of her pussy. "I want you to spank me," she said.

Transfixed by the movement of her naked flesh and that wondrous ass, he walked up behind her. Impulsively, he cupped her buttocks. *Sweet Nirvana!* He thought.

He wanted to fuck her so hard, right then and there, but decided to play along. Holding up a hand at the ready, he looked at her for his queue.

"Spank me," she said. So he did, with a light slap. First one cheek, and then the other. He really enjoyed how her firm buttocks moved when he did so.

She shuddered, and said, "Harder! And don't be a pussy about it!"

Well, okay then, he thought.

He did, this Hakime a little harder, and using his full palm, not just the fingers. She yelped, and he found his hand actually stung.

"More!"

"Yes, Ma'am!" he said, and did so. Over and over he smacked her lovely ass, until it progressed to a full on spanking. Each time she yelped, or groaned. She even gritted her teeth to keep from screaming out, but that didn't last long as he kept at it. Smack, smack, smack.

She raised a hand. "Okay, okay," she panted. "Stop!"

Disappointed, he did. "Did I hurt you?" He hadn't wanted to have this kinky little exercise end due to him being overzealous.

"No," she said. "Not yet." She grinned evilly.

Hakim nearly cam in his pants from her expression alone.

"Not yet?" he echoed, oblivious to the meaning, but wanting to know more, all the same.

She pointed to one of the carts, which was full of thick hardcovers. "Grab a classic."

Obeying, he walked over to it, feeling his hard-on chaff roughly against the inside of his pants. Not trying to be subtle, he shifted his dick over with one hand, as he picked out a book from the cart selection with the other.

"How about this?" he asked.

Her panting had lessened, and she was using a hand to reach around and massage her the bright red skin of her dark ass. "Is it a classic?"

"Classic?" he looked. "Uh, it's about medicine or something."

She had moved a finger over her raw pussy, and she flinched with ecstasy at the painful touch. "No, not that one. Get something good, something that has meaning."

Confused at the request, but not wanting to question it for fear of putting a sudden end to this wonderful encounter, he picked out another book.

"The Complete Dickens Collection," he said hefting the large tome. It was thick and weight a good couple pounds.

She nodded with a smile, one finger teasing the wetness of her pussy around. "That will do. It has Dick in it."

Hakim actually laughed out loud. She laughed too.

He was not going to argue this, so he stood behind her, and to one side. *Fuck she looks hot*, he thought. She had braced her arms on the desk again, in preparation of the wonderful pain.

He gripped the big book with both hands, and hoisted it over one shoulder. This view accentuated the wonder curve of her buttock muscles, and again, his boner begged to be released.

"I'd really like to fuck the hell out you right now," he admitted. He almost regretted blurting it out, but God damn this chick looked fuckable as all hell.

She winked at him over shoulder, "Soon. Very, very soon. But first, do this to me. I need it to get going." She smiled.

God, I am one lucky guy, he thought. His face actually hurt from grinning so much.

"Ready?" he asked.

Without saying anything, she faced forward again, and nodded her head vigorously. She was psyching herself up.

She took a deep breath. He took a deep breath.

He swung hard aiming at the curving muscle of her ass, directly from behind.

She grunted, but gritted her teeth. And he smacked her again, then again. Over and over.

At first, she kept the noise she made to a minimum, but as he kept spanking her with the big book, she started to get louder. Soon, she was almost shouting with each and every smack.

Her body would even quiver with the anticipation of each hit. But she didn't tell him to stop. She only flinched, making her small pert breasts jiggle.

Eventually, she raised her hand again, and he stopped. She was breathing too hard from the shrieking to say anything at first. He lowered the book, and waited. His cock throbbed in his pants for her. She looked so damned fuckable.

"Okay, okay!" she was gasping. "Now get some Shakespeare!"

Was she kidding? When were they gonna fuck? He thought, incredulous. But he did as he was asked. When a hot, naked chick, who is bent over begging to be spanked and spanked hard, asks you to do something that turns her on even more; you did it, damn it!

He got it, and it was twice the size of the other. His eyes widened as he hefted it. "Are you sure?" he asked, concerned.

"Yeah," she said, nodding quickly. "Do it now before I change my mind! Spank my ass with it!"

Again, he smacked her, again she shrieked with pain and delight. He repeated this over and over until he was certain the bright red skin on her ass was going to burst from all that punishment.

This Hakime, she did not last as long as previously before she raised her hand, and he stopped.

He found his fingers actually started to hurt, where they got caught between the book and the firm flesh of her ass. He could even see they made a couple of impressions on her lovely skin. Red on red.

She was gasping for air, and her whole body quivered and shook. *Is she having an orgasm?* He thought.

"Okay," she said, gulping in air. "Pants off!"

He did not require any further coaxing, and his shoes, pants and boxers flew in different directions within seconds.

Bent over as she was, her pussy was pushed out, glistening. He could see she was very wet, to the point where it dribbled all down her lips, and partially down one of her inner thighs.

His mouth watered just looking at it.

"Eat me," she said. "Lick me all up."

All right! He got down on his knees, lightly gripped her red ass, spreading the rounded cheeks a little. Then he licked her; nice and long at first, from the bottom to the top. *Or was it top to the bottom from this angle?* he thought.

She tasted incredible and he told her so. Her pussy was sopping wet from being turned on so much from the spanking. He could feel the heat of the blood brought so close to the surface of her red skin, rubbing against his cheeks and chin. He licked her for several long tasty minutes until she was moaning again. He could feel her wetness all over his chin, and some dribbled a little down his throat.

Careful, he sucked out her clit between his lips, and it was his turn to use his tongue for flickering.

Malaya arched her back, groaning. Occasionally she pushed back so his face was forced deeper inside her incredible wetness, and he nearly went mad with the feeling of it.

He worked on her pussy like this for a long Hakime, sucking up her lips so their soft folds slipped in gently between his teeth. Her entire body shuddered and quaked. Eventually, she couldn't handle any more, and said, "Fuck me!"

She looked over her shoulder at his eyes that peeked over the curvature of her ass. "Fuck me with your Dickens!"

He stood up, grabbed his dick (or was it Dickens?) which was now pulsating, and put his other hand on her ass. Then, very slowly, he slide his prick into her. He bite his bottom lip because he nearly lost it right there.

Taking a moment to gather himself, he then slid his entire length into her. He gasped. She felt so damn good; very hot, and very wet. Then he slid back his length until it was nearly out, and slammed it back in all the way. She grunted. He did it again. And again.

He pumped her, hard as she had asked him to. He marvelled at the the bright redness of her ass, and gazed down appreciatively at her little pink ass-hole. He rubbed at her asshole with a thumb, all the while not stopping with his rhythm. Her flesh jiggled, but was so firm it barely moved.

She tossed her head back and forth, occasionally arching her back all the way so he could reach around and squeeze her firm little tits. At one point he pulled her back by the elbows so she was almost standing up straight, and slammed her pussy harder and harder.

Soon, after all that had happened, and with the incredible sensation of being finally inside her, he couldn't hold it any longer.

"Ah, fuck!" he groaned loudly.

She instinctively knew what this meant, reached back and gently pushed at his stomach so he eased out of her. Her pussy made wet noises as if in protest.

Spinning around, she dropped to her knees in front of him, and as he stroked his shaft, she slurped his dick into her hot mouth. She sucked furiously until he practically screamed as he came into her mouth.

Somehow she managed to chuckle while sucking him off. His hips bucked with his orgasm, as if he was fucking her mouth. When he was nearly spent, she swallowed loudly, never letting his cock out of her mouth. He sagged against the desk as she continued to nurse his load.

"Whoa," he said. He could feel his body was covered in sweat from such wonderful exertion.

Malaya pulled his cock out of her mouth with a wet pop, and said, "Well, Hakim. Thanks for the quickie. This really topped off my day." She smiled and returned to sucking him dry.

Chuckling, Hakim couldn't agree more!

END

Her Boss

When Audell answered his front door, the stunning young woman standing outside literally rendered him speechless.

She was young, and amazingly curvy; like a walking hourglass. But what really caught his gaze was her incredible bosom. Big breasts that seemed to be nearly bursting out of the skin tight t-shirt she wore.

My God, he suddenly thought, *those must be forty-four double-dees!*

Thanks to her youthful age, her breasts easily defied gravity by barely sagging.

"Hi," she said, cheerfully. "I'm Ishawna. The house cleaning agency sent me. Are you Audell?"

Man the torpedoes, he thought. *She must stack those on shelves at night.*

His mouth dropped, but managed to gather his senses and say, "Oh, yes. I am. Please come in." He stood back and she walked past him into the foyer. He got a nice whiff of her perfume, and repressed a shudder.

"Nice place you have," she said. As she looked around, he sneaked a glance at her legs. She was wearing very short shorts, that only came down to her upper thigh. If this was a standard issue housekeeper uniform then he was an instant fan. Her legs were muscular. He wondered how smooth they would feel if he ran his hands over them.

She looked back at him, "So, where would you like me to start?"

"Uh, yeah. Right," he said, barely managing to tear his gaze from hers. She was watching him rather intensely.

"Well, you can start wherever you like. It's a big house and is quite the handful."

"Are you?" she asked, one cute eyebrow bending in question.

"Am I what?"

"A handful?" her smile turned into a grin.

Holy shit, he thought. *Is this little goddess actually flirting with me?*

Still, she grinned at him, and that eyebrow remained crooked.

No, he thought. *She's just teasing me. I'm so out of practise with women my hopes have started to blur reality. No way as young and hot as this would be into a middle aged frump like me.*

She turned and looked around. Audell got a side profile of those breasts, and that incredible bouncy ass, which nearly caused him to faint.

"I'll start with the upstairs," she said. "Then I'll work my way down slowly." She eyed him. "Always works for me."

"Okay," Audell said, trying to regain his senses and not make a fool of himself. "I have to go meet a friend for a bit. Should be back in a couple of hours."

She gave him that wicked grin again, and said, "Oh, don't have to much fun now."

He left the house, feeling like all he really wanted to do was stay home and watch her glide around. *Ah well*, he thought to himself. *Some young buck must be tapping that without any appreciation of just how God damned lucky his his. Little bastard.*

He drove across town to his favourite watering hole, The Richman's Pub. After parking in his usual spot he went inside to find that his drinking buddy, Kamar had already arrived. He had claimed a table near the waitress serving section of the bar, where the pretty servers line up to get their orders. Making for nice viewing while they chatted.

"Hey, what's up?" Kamar said. He had one eye on his depleting beer, and the other on the backside of one of the waitress standing across from them.

"I should be asking you that," said Audell with grin.

"Nothing that the ladies can't be taught to handle," said Kamar, and they both laughed. "So, anything new in the wonderfully dull world that is Audell?" Kamar had always teased him about woeful lack of dating since his divorce. Audell just wasn't ready, Kamar felt it was his obligation as a single male, to go forth and get into the panties of any female that would let him.

"Well, you're not gonna believe this, but I met a woman."

Kamar leaned forward, suddenly intrigued. "Oh, share with me buddy, who is she?"

"The new housekeeper."

"The new housekeeper? Oh, wow. Robbing the cradle?" he grinned.

Audell held up his hands, "Nah, she's twenty or so, she's not really a kid."

"That makes it all the better, dear boy!"

They stopped talking so as to smile at the cute waitress who dropped off Audell's beer. Their eyes were on her ass as she walked away, then clinked their glasses together in mutual appreciation.

Kamar raised an eyebrow at him. "Well, tell me. What does this housekeeper look like?"

So Audell described her in minute detail, sparing nothing. He sounded like a teenager with his lewd language, but he was with his friend, and guys always talked that way. Especially when there wasn't any females around to protest.

But when he described Ishawna's most noticeable assets, her breasts, Kamar's face dropped.

"Wait," Kamar said, "That sounds familiar. She's from a cleaning service?"

"Yeah," Audell tried to hide the concern in his voice. Why would Ishawna be familiar to Kamar?

Suddenly, Kamar threw his head back and laughed. "Oh, man that is rich! You are one lucky son of a bitch, you know that?"

"What? Why?"

"Let me guess, is her name Ishawna?"

Audell was dumbstruck. "Yeah, Ishawna. How the hell did you know?"

Kamar was still laughing, tears rolling down his face.

"Come on, tell me, dammit!" said Audell, growing very annoyed.

Kamar settled down, and when he stopped laughing he looked at Audell with a big, shit eating grin. "Buddy, you hit the jackpot. Remember Tyrese? That guy we played golf with during the summer?"

"Yeah, so?"

"Well, he told me about this hot as hell little housekeeper he once hired, who had tits to die for. Her name was Ishawna, too."

"No, way. Can't be the same one."

"I don't doubt that it is. I mean what are the odds. Same age, same body, same general neighbourhood. And most importantly, same giant gravity defying tits!"

Audell felt himself growing disappointed. "So, what happened?"

Kamar sipped his beer, "What do think what happened? The fucked like rabbits."

"I don't believe it."

"Oh, it's true alright. And she was a complete sex fiend, too. The best kind. She'd come over, and he'd leave to run some errands. Then, when he came back they'd fuck. And fuck a lot, from what I remember him saying."

"Really?"

"He said she'd ride him all night, and suck him dry. Suck him dry! Now where can I get a girl like that?" Kamar grinned. "Oh, I know. At your place."

"Okay, settle down. Fine, so what if it's her. They still a couple?"

Kamar almost spat out a mouthful of beer, "Hell no. Purely sexual. The best kind there is, as we both know. Just wanted him for the sex. But, they stopped a while ago."

"Why's that?"

"On account of he got married to some chick from his office. Now he uses a different housekeeper, some old woman who looks like a Russian shot-putter." Kamar shrugged. "No chance of him diddling that."

Audell felt hopeful. "So, they, like, stopped. Completely?"

"Yes, and you know what the best part of all this is? Know what he said about her?"

Audell was a little sceptical. Perhaps he didn't want to hear this part, but he relented. "What?"

"She digs older guys. Much older. Likes them for the experience they have, and the fact the tend to last longer than younger ones. Well, most, anyway."

Audell felt his spirits raise with this news. *So, maybe she was actually flirting with me, and it wasn't just my imagination.*

Still...

"Man," Audell said, shaking his head in disbelief. "She is one *hot* little lady."

"I know it's been a while for you," Kamar said. "Quite a while, but what better way to get back into the game than with a young sex starved filly who loves older men? And she has a history of bonking the ones she cleans houses for." Kamar's face was one big smile. "I think you may get a surprise when you get home tonight."

Audell was doubtful, but felt his pulse quicken at the prospect.

Later, he cut things short with Kamar and headed home. He tried to keep his expectations at zero. But inward, he cursed himself. *I always do this. Get my hopes up. Nothing is going to happen except she'll leave and I'll just whack off as usual.*

He entered his house, and looked around. He found Ishawna in the kitchen, cleaning up some dishes he had left there to fossilize with yesterday's food. She turned at the sound of him entering, and immediately lit up in a big smile.

"Welcome back," she said, hanging a dishtowel. She leaned against the counter so one hip stuck outward. She looked incredibly sexy that way.

He caught himself staring at her, looking over her lovely form. She didn't seem to mind, in fact she appeared to enjoy his perusal.

"Everything go okay with the cleaning?" he asked.

"Oh, yeah. No problem at all," she locked her gaze onto him. "Just like its owner."

Audell felt a hard-on start to roar to life in his jeans.

"So," he said.

"So," she said, smiling.

"I meant to ask you, have you had much experience house cleaning before this?" he said, trying to act casual about it.

She frowned a little, making her look all the more appealing. "Yeah, I cleaned a house regularly last summer. Did it for a while. But not anymore."

Well, well, well, he thought. I*t is her!* He felt his pulse begin to race.

"Ah, cool," he said.

"I really missed that, too. I really enjoyed it," she said.

"The house?" he said.

"Well, yes, I miss them. But I missed its owner even more," she said, her big brown eyes locked onto his own.

"Why's that?" he almost whispered.

"He'd teach me things. I like to be taught, by older men in particular. Older guys know so many wonderful things."

Suddenly, she closed the distance between them, and put her hands on his shoulders. She was firmly pressed up against him, huge tits mashed against his stomach. Her tummy was also planted firmly against the bulge in his pants, which was growing rapidly.

"Well, you're an older man, more experienced in many things than I," she batted her eyelashes at him. "What would you like to teach me?"

But before he could respond, she kissed him. The smell and taste of her nearly overwhelmed him, but he kissed her back, and with equal passion. Their tongues wrestled, probing the other's mouth.

They necked for several minutes, until she took her hand and grabbed his crotch. He liked it, and ground against her.

Got to get the girl into a bed, and fast, he thought.

His face must of betrayed his thoughts, because Ishawna said, "I noticed you have a downstairs guest room."

"Yeah," he said.

"Lets fuck there." She grinned wickedly at him.

He liked the way she thought.

She took him by the hand and led him through the house and into the back guest room.

Then, unbidden, she peeled off her t-shirt, revealing her stunningly full cleavage. It was as if her breasts were seconds away from bursting from their confines of the bra.

He stood memorized as she reached back and fiddle with the clasp. She watched him, enjoying his lustful look. Then, she shrugged off the bra and tossed it to the floor.

Her tits were incredible, only sagging slightly now that they were free. Her skin was a beautiful creamy brown. Each tit was bigger than his own head. He felt himself start to drool.

Still keeping an eye on his expression, she then wiggled out of her shorts, and thong underwear, tossing those aside, too. She stood before him, completely naked and looking like a Greek Goddess of Fuckability.

She walked forward, breasts jiggling hypnotically, and grabbed at his own shirt. He only flinched just slightly, as if his brain was only now catching up with unfolding events, but he smiled and yielded.

He chuckled and raised his arms so she could pull the it off of him.

Ishawna ran her hands over his chest, then sucked on one of his nipples, teething it. Then she kissed the other, flicking it with her tongue. He managed to work his hands up between them to cup her ample breasts, squeezing them.

She then grabbed at his belt and undid it with a playful grunt. He smiled and let her work at it. When unbuckled, she unzipped his fly, then squatted down in front of him, pulling his pants down. She managed to work them to his hips, and with one final tug, yanked them down to his knees.

She pulled off his shoes, and then aided him in removing his pants from his ankles. She then turned her attention to the now erect penis in front of her, demanding attention.

Grabbing it eagerly, she stroking it up and down, marvelling at its thickness, and heft. She then put it in her mouth, and started to suck. Looking down at her, all he could see was the back of her head, as she worked her mouth up and down his length with loud slurping gusto.

One of his hands was on the back of her head, holding her ponytail, almost as if to ensure she didn't get away. Slowly stroking him she followed her hands up and down with her mouth, sucking with determination. He really liked it when she partially gagged on his cock.

Up and down she worked him. Long minutes of concentrated effort, with her mouth made his dick glisten, creating a slight foam at its base. Some spit eventually dribbled down to his balls to dangle there.

With one final suck, she kept stroking his shaft, and said, "Let's move to that chair. I want to ride you like a bucking bronco." He eagerly nodded in agreement. She stood, and while guiding him by his dick, gently pulled him over to easy chair in the corner of the room.

She made him sit facing towards her. She placed a hand on either side of his face then she stepped forward a little and pressed his face into her pussy.

He kissed it hungrily, licking and sucking the length of her. She held him there for a very long time, enjoying the sensation. He reached around to grab her round ass cheeks with both hands and squeezed. Occasionally she would grind her pussy in his face, and he enjoyed hearing, and feeling, her moan.

She then turned around and straddled him. Squatting down, she took his dick and guided it inside herself, until she had slid down his full-length. Putting her hands on his thighs, just above the knees, she started to move up and down. He grabbed at her ass while leaning backwards, helping her with the movements.

She rode him, moving slowly at first until she found a wonderful rhythm. Then she started to go faster, always making sure she slid up his entire length, almost until it seemed he would escape her velvety grip, only to suddenly slam down and smack loudly against the flesh of his legs. Many minutes past like this. Riding him on and on.

After a while she switch the position around, so they were facing each other. He smiled at her, as she did so. But his focus quickly switched to her ample breasts. As she slammed up and down, he gripped her tits and sucked and teethed on their nipples. Sometimes he would bury his face between them, until they smothered him. They were so huge!

She looked down at him and said, "I've taught you something, now maybe you can teach me in something in return," she said with a wicked smile.

Again, they switched up positions, this time she knelt on the chair, leaning over it, and he got behind her. Audell took his hard cock and bounced it playfully off her ass several times. He watched as her buttocks jiggled. Then he guided it down, and very slowly slipped all of it into her waiting pussy. She gasped with the sudden penetration.

Her ass was absolutely perfectly shaped; like a plump inverted heart pressed against his hips. It was so firm, it barely jiggled when he pumped hard against it. He got even more aroused just running his hands around its amazing flesh, over and over.

Her pussy was incredibly slick now, as he had worked her up into a lather. His dick slide in an out of her, causing her pussy to make wet noises. "It's talking to you," she said, looking over her should at him, breathing heavy.

He smacked her ass in response. "I'm teaching it a lesson," he said, smiling.

He pumped her for what seemed like hours, but it was never really long enough. Then he withdrew from her, and turned her around so she was laying partially on the chair, legs outstretched. She smiled up at him, and rubbed at her clit. "Fuck me," she said. "Teach me another lesson!"

He hovered between her widely outstretched legs and suddenly jammed his cock down deep inside her waiting pussy.

They both grunted with the roughness of the motion. Then, bracing arms on the chair, he began moving his hips up and down. He pulled himself out almost the full length of his dick, until it nearly unsheathed itself, and then slamming it back down with pleasurable force.

Over and over he did this, getting faster and faster. She moaned with each pelvic thrust. Long wonderful minutes passed as he slammed her pussy again and again. Eventually, the intensity got to be so much Ishawna's eyes rolled upwards showing only their browns.

Then he slowed, making easy gyrating motions with his hips but could not keep up the relentless pace. With both the feeling of the rubbing wet friction inside her, and seeing her face grimace with the concentrated effort of their passion, he found himself about to orgasm.

"I'm gonna cum!" he finally gasped.

Quickly, Ishawna pushed him back, unsheathing him from her.

He stood before her, stroking his cock vigorously. Sitting on the edge of the chair, she leaned forward so she could place the bottom of her open mouth against the base of his prick. Her tongue tickled at it eagerly, and her eyes stared up at him with hunger.

He stroked faster, and soon came with a loud moan. His semen spat out all over her; hot squirts into her mouth which slid down her tongue and pooled at the back of her throat. Over her face in long sticky strands that splayed across her cheeks and forehead. In the corner of one eye, down her chin, and he even got some in her hair.

As he sagged with completion, and she made a dramatic show of swallowing.

She smacked her mouth, and rolled her tongue around her lips, getting every brown bit. A long thick strand still hung from her chin as she grinned widely at him.

She then grabbed his dick, and sucked it as his erection faded, nursing the last of his load.

He held her head in his hands, feeling the slow motion of her movements, and he grinned up at the ceiling feeling wonderful.

I think I'm going to need a housekeeper more often! He thought.

END

His Big Package

"I've had it with cheating men!" cried Amara into her cell phone.

Her friend, Kisha, who was on the receiving end of this declaration, tried to calm her down. "Oh, Amara, honey," she said. "They're not all bad. Some of them are genuinely cowed enough to know they shouldn't mess with alpha females like us."

Neither woman felt such a statement was close to the truth, but it certainly helped Amara a little to think it was. At least for the moment. Was she ready to give up on men all together?

Amara paced her apartment living room. "I don't care to find out anymore. So many games, so many lies. A woman can't get anything honest from someone who owns a penis. They just can't be trusted."

She had reason to be angry. Mike, her boyfriend... ex-boyfriend... had just admitted to her, not fifteen minutes ago, that he had been unfaithful to her for the last two months of their relationship. With some waitress at a bar he frequented.

The coward had told her over the phone, too. He didn't have the nerve, or the balls, to tell her to her face. She would have liked to have punched him! Or at least scratched his eyes out.

Kisha continued to try and calm her friend down. "Yeah, they're scum. They can't be trusted. Maybe you should just, I dunno, maybe take a break from serious relationships for a little bit. I know this just happened and all, but maybe this was for the best."

Amara had paced into the bedroom and caught her reflection in the closet mirror. She was still in a bathrobe, having showered in preparation for going out with Antonne that evening. She gave her body an appraising once over. She was hot dammit! Why would any man in his right mind even entertain the idea of screwing around behind her back? Especially *this* lovely back! She turned and lifted up the robe exposing a very firm, and pleasant round shaped ass.

No more of this honey-dew for him!

"I know, I know," Amara said. "It just hurts. I thought we had something truly meaningful. But I guess it wasn't meaningful enough." She gave her own ass a smack and was pleased that it barely shook. "Maybe I should just pick up some random piece of meat at the bar and screw the hell out of it."

"Yes!" Kisha shouted. "Nothing better than cheap meaningless sex with a stranger to help you get through times of trouble."

Just then the downstairs buzzer rang.

"Who's that?" asked Kisha.

"Oh, shoot. I was expecting a package delivered today for work." Mike had called her right after she got the a call-confirmation, asking if she would be home. She buzzed in whoever it was without answering.

"Wait a second, sister," said Kisha, conspiratorially. "What if he's a hunk?"

Amara scoffed. "No, it's always this little fat guy who smells of sweat and cheese."

"You should *do* him!"

"No way!" Amara shuddered. Just the thought of it made her skin crawl.

"Or, it could be someone different. A moonlighting underwear model."

Amara's brow furrowed. "Wow, you have quite the imagination. Well, if that were the case, he'd get one hell of a tip outta me, tonight."

"That a girl!" cried Kisha.

Amara was only half joking. It would take a lot to get her to indulge in a casual quickie with a stranger.

There was a knock at the door. Amara took a moment to look herself over in the living room mirror. The robe hung half open, so she cinched it closed. It accentuated her voluptuous breasts. Her muscular legs were bare for all to see. The robe only just covered her ass. She hadn't put on any underwear after she finished showering, and there certainly wasn't any time now to put some on.

I do look damn sexy, though, she thought to herself. At least mister chubby from the pizza place will get a little bit of an eye full.

While she walked to the door, Kisha was chanting in the phone, "Hot sex! Hot sex! Hot sex!"

Amara could only roll her eyes. As if.

She peered through the peek hole.

A tall dashing hunk of a black man was standing out there. Holding a boxed package. Her boxed package.

"Uh," was all Amara was able to say.

Kisha immediately pounced. "What? WHAT?!"

Amara found herself whispering, her eye glued to the hole, drinking in the beefcake outside. "It's not the usual guy. He's..." *Gorgeous.*

"So? Is he handsome, or just handsome enough?" asked Kisha, intrigued with her friend's change of tone. "Either will do for now."

Amara realized she had been staring at him entirely too long. She took a deep breath and opened the door.

The peephole view did not do this walking Greek God justice. Tall, chiseled features, and perfectly muscled, he gave Amara a pearly white smile.

"Hi," he said. "I have a package delivery for a Amara?"

Amara was momentarily speechless. She was also alarmed to feel a dampness grow between her upper thighs.

"Yeah," she managed to stammer smiling, still a little shocked. She stepped back, letting him inside. She closed the door behind him.

She had forgotten her cell phone was in her free hand, until she dimly heard Kisha cry out: "Do him! Screw his brains out! Give him a tip he'll never forget!"

Amara quickly hung up. The delivery boy... man... stud, crooked a questioning eyebrow. She managed not to blush. "My friend is being annoying," she finally said, and immediately felt ridiculous.

He continued smiling politely, "Our delivery service has that effect on folks." His eyes were incredibly piercing, and they glanced down at her robe, and then at her legs before quickly returning to her eyes again.

She was surprised to find herself thrilled at this.

"You're not the usual courier guy."

"Oh, you probably get Peter," his voice was deep, confident. The kind you wouldn't mind having whispering instructions in your ear. "He called in sick so I had to pick up the slack."

She nodded, dully. This guy was a lot to take in. She suddenly found herself wondering just how much that would be, and in how many positions. "I've never seen you before. Are you new there?"

"New? Oh, more than that. I'm the owner."

She looked down at the company name on the package. It said Germain's Package Delivery Service. "You're Germain?" she said, incredulous.

"The big boss man himself," he said with a confident grin.

She found she was most definitely horny, now. Maybe there was a package he could delivery for her, and not the one in his hands.

She was struck with a strong impulse and felt an overwhelming urge to act on it. Kisha was right. Meaningless sex with a stranger could be exactly what she needs right now. Especially with this particular handsome stranger.

"Oh, uh, please bring it in the living room," she said, walking away from him. He more or less had to follow. As she turned she sneaked a look at his wedding finger. Barren.

Good.

She also noted his eyes fell on her butt as she talked to him over her shoulder.

"Right over there, please," she pointed at the big coffee table which was between the couch and the easy chair. There was a plate of warmed up pizza she was nibbling on, sitting on the table.

Germain gave a short nod to her as he passed. She inhaled his wake as he did so, and liked the hint of his cologne, and the slight tinge of sweat. Most likely from working hard most of the night.

She yearned to make him sweat some more.

He placed the package on the table, and as he turned toward her, she quickly undid her robes, and let them fall to the floor. She put her hands on her curvy hips and bent a knee slighting for enticing emphasis.

He froze, eyes locked on her naked form. She was sexy as all hell, and she could see he thought the same.

"Well, Germain of Germain's Delivery Service," she said, with fire in her eyes, and a seductive

tone in her voice. "I have a way I can pay you properly for that package."

His jaw dropped, and his eyes roved over her. He was appropriately shell shocked, and took several moments to compose himself.

Who could blame him?

"I, uh..." he stammered.

Deciding to take her initiative even further she didn't want him to have to decide on his own. She walked forward, breasts jiggling hypnotically, and grabbed at his t-shirt. He only flinched just slightly, as if his brain was only now catching up with unfolding events, but he smiled and yielded.

He chuckled and raised his arms so she could pull the it off of him.

His chest did not disappoint. Ridged muscles lined his body and stomach. His pectorals were the size of dinner plates and his arms were hard as tempered steel, and almost as thick as her own thighs.

Amara ran her hands over his barrelled chest. "You lift a lot of heavy packages to get a body like that?" she asked teasingly.

"Something like that," he said. His hands rubbed her shoulders, and up and down her arms. Then he cupped her ample breasts, squeezing them. She found his hands were calloused and strong, just the way she liked them.

She grabbed at his belt and undid it with a playful grunt. He smiled and let her work at it. When unbuckled, she unzipped his fly, then squatted down in front of him, pulling his pants down. She managed to work them to his hips, and with one final tug, yanked them down to his knees.

It was then that a huge dick popped out of them, partially engorged. The sudden motion of the pants had freed this large piece of meat from its lair, and it swung out and hit her in the side of the nose.

"Oh, my God!" She gasped. He smiled down at her. She blinked in astonishment. "I don't remember ordering this!" She giggled, amazed.

"It's an extra service. For hot, sexy customers only," he said.

She pulled off his shoes, and then aided him in removing his pants from his ankles. She then turned her attention to the now large erect penis in front of her, demanding attention.

Grabbing it eagerly, she stroking it up and down, marvelling at its thickness, and heft. Stealing her courage, she then put it in her mouth, and started to suck. It was large, but she had managed this size before.

Germain sighed with the sudden feel of her warm wet mouth on his prick, and the feel of her lips moving up and down his shaft. Because of his size, the sound of her slurping and occasional gagging was more prominent.

Up and down she worked him. Long minutes of concentrated effort, with her mouth made his dick glisten with her spit, creating a slight foam at its base. Some spit eventually dribbled down to his balls to dangle there in an elastic string.

Satisfied she had properly welcomed him into her home, she leaned back a bit for a breather, and gasped.

She motioned to the easy chair, "Sit down. I have an idea."

"I like your ideas so far," he said with wide appreciative eyes. He did as he was told.

She turned to the still-hot pizza slice on the table and stuck her fingers in it. As she tried to pick at a ring of green pepper she squealed girlishly from its heat. Finding one that suited her needs, she turned towards him, and his eyes widened at what she had in mind.

Gingerly, she broke it at one point, then wrapped the green pepper around the base of his thick cock. Because he was so well shaved, it rested against his skin and he hissed slightly, but not with great pain.

"You okay?" she asked coyly.

"Oh, yeah," he said through gritted teeth. "I knew my customers were hot but not *this* hot."

She grinned up at him, then swirled her tongue around his prick. She took his dick in her mouth, and slowly worked her way down his length, occasionally pausing to wiggle her head back and forth to help it past the hook at the back of her throat. He gasped, as her tongue poked out of the bottom of her gaping mouth. His girth had forced her mouth wide, stretching her lips around him. Spittle gathered in sticky strands at the corners.

With amazing patience, she neither gagged, or pulled back. She gazed up at him with big eyes, and her tongue prodded the green pepper until she managed to catch it. Then, very slowly, she slid back up his length, green pepper in tow.

Sucking him at the tip, the green pepper dangled from her mouth. Then she leaned back, plucking it in her fingers and smiling at him triumphantly.

"Impressive!" He said, laughing. "My turn to do a trick."

He eased her up off her knees, and had her sit in the easy chair, this time. She spread her legs by hooking her knees over the arms, exposing her very well shaved, and *very* wet pussy to him. She rubbed at her clit playfully.

"Do as you please, delivery boy," she said while teething the tip of one of her fingers.

"Oh, I will," Germain returned. With one finger he dipped into the tomato sauce of the pizza slice. Careful to get enough, he then slowly spread it around her pussy, smearing it completely with sauce.

It was her turn to grit her teeth from the heat, as he worked his fingers around her clit. Then he leaned forward, and with strong hands firmly holding her legs wide at the thighs, he started to lick.

Up and down, then all around, he licked and slurped. When a little sauce dripped down into the slight hollow at her asshole, he slurped it up. He then stayed there, rimming her asshole with his tongue.

Amara gasped with pleasure, squeezing her tits, pinching at their erect nipples.

Then he returned his attention to her pussy, taking long deliberate licks, making sure he wasn't finished until it was completely cleaned of tomato sauce.

Germain grinned up at her and said, "My special sauce never tasted so damn good."

She smiled back and said, "Glad to finally be on your menu."

He then stood, cock hard and ready. He leaned forward, so he was hovering over her, and bent his dick as far as it would go. He stuck his prick into her waiting pussy. She gasped, and grabbed onto his hips. He paused, and said, "Can I make an express delivery, ma'am?"

"Please do!" Amara said.

And with that, he suddenly slammed the entire length of his long dick deep inside her. She gasped with the hard penetration. He then lifted his ass up again, so his entire length was nearly unsheathed from her, and slammed it down again.

Over and over he did this, getting faster and faster. She moaned with each pelvic thrust. Long wonderful minutes passed as he slammed her pussy again and again. Eventually, the intensity got to be so much Amara's eyes rolled upwards showing only their whites.

He reached around her neck and pulled against her head slightly, so as to cut off some of the circulation. She gasped for air while he continued his relentless hammering. He eased off her head only when she seemed close to passing out.

Then he slowed, making easy gyrating motions with his hips. Germain wanted to give her a little time to recover before giving her what was about to happen next.

When she seemed okay, he slipped out of her and her pussy gave a wet fart. He then turned her around and pushed her on the chair so her upper body leaning against the back of it. Her beautiful tits hung down over the back edge. Germain perched behind her, and smacked her incredible ass. It shook only slightly, being so firm.

Then he eased his dick into her pussy again, which was now sopping wet. Making sure Amara was firmly pressed up against the chair, hands holding her hips tightly, he began to pump back and forth. Each time he slammed her ass she grunted with the force of it. He could feel the bottom of his cock rub hard against the inside of her and he knew she felt it, too.

Again, he was relentless in his pounding. Over and over. She gasped and moaned and dug her fingers into the chair. She was almost certain he was going to pound her straight through it.

The apartment filled with the ceaseless smacking of flesh on flesh. Punctuated with their moans of pleasure.

Eventually, he grabbed her arms, and pulled them back by the elbows, forcing her to arch her back. Her long dark hair dangled down to almost brush against the small of her back, and shook with each hard thrust. He began to slam against her even harder and she moaned more deeply.

On the other side of the living room was a mirror. In the reflection, he could see her firm breasts moving with the harsh pounding rhythm. Her mouth was open, eyes were closed, and her brow was furrowed with gritting pleasure.

Over and over; again and again Germain tapped that ass, until he could see that she was getting red where their flesh smacked against one an other.

He could not keep up this relentless pace. With both the feeling of him rubbing wetly inside her, and seeing her wonderfully firm flesh vibrating with his effort, he found himself about to explode.

"I'm gonna cum!" he practically shouted.

Quickly, Amara pulled her body forward so as to unsheathe his dick from her, and she spun around. He stood, stroking his cock vigorously. She placed the bottom of her open mouth against the base of his prick. Her tongue tickled at it eagerly, and her eyes stared up at him with hunger.

He stroked faster, and soon exploded with a loud moan. He semen spat out all over her; many hot squirts into her mouth which slid down her tongue and pooled at the back of her throat. Over her face in long sticky strands that splayed across her cheeks and forehead. In the corner of one eye, down her chin, and he even got some in her dark hair.

As he sagged with completion, she made a dramatic show of swallowing.

She smacked her mouth, and rolled her tongue around her lips, getting every white bit. A long thick strand still hung from her chin as she grinned widely at him.

She then grabbed his dick again, and sucked it as his erection faded, nursing the last of his load. She wanted every little bit of that special sauce.

It was while she was doing this, and looking up at the exhausted pleasure in his face, that she made a wondrous conclusion:

She needed to get courier service more often, dammit!

END

Wild Ride

Delonda faced a long, and boring drive through the countryside as she headed south to visit family for the holidays.

She found the radio annoying as it continuously played sappy love songs over and over, so she just turned off. Unfortunately, this left her with her thoughts and memories of her recently failed relationship with her ex-husband, Caleb. They had been married for less than three years but she knew it had been doomed from the start. The passion that initially attracted them to each other faded quickly and they simply fell into the routine of having each other around.

And it was passion she wanted more of in her life, and since there was no more with Caleb she made the painful decision of cancelling the whole thing. They separated only last month and filed the divorce paperwork. And despite being amicable it was still quite stressful.

The early morning sun gave an orange hew to the sky, and tinged the countless trees that strobe by her on both sides of the winding country road. There was very little traffic, which was why she purposely took this more scenic route to her parents house several states away. She did not mind peacefulness but having Caleb around for so many years she found a lack of another person's presence daunting.

She had no one else in her life at the moment to fill the void. Neither she nor Caleb were unfaithful to the other during their failing relationship. And having only just recently separated she had neither the time, nor the will to find someone.

What she really craved with someone to find her. A distraction of the momentary kind. She did not think she had the emotional toolkit to deal with anything too heavy.

"I just need a man," she said to herself. She laughed at the absurdity of that declaration. She wasn't gonna find anyone at her parent's house, that was for certain. And she sure as hell didn't think anyone was waiting for her out here, in the middle of nowhere.

She peered up at the mountains, each covered with an apron of thick forest, that she slowly past by. "Nope," she said. "Only thing out here are mountain men and Bigfoot. And both would be too smelly for my taste."

As her mind wandered, she concentrated less on the road. At a particularly sharp turn, a figure suddenly appeared directly in front of her. A *man*, standing dangerously close to the edge of the turn in the road.

She yelped, and yanked at the wheel, swerving to avoid him. Her car fish tailed and she fought to control it. Pumping the brakes she managed to avoid flying off the road and into the trees. Always a cautious driver, she had not been travelling too fast and she skidded to a stop directly on the meridian facing the direction she had been coming from.

Her fingers were dug into the steering wheel and her hair was now in her face, which puffed out as she breathed heavily.

Is that what it's like to almost die?, she thought. She barked out a laugh, still in shock.

It was only after a few moments of recovering that she realized someone was running toward the car. The stupid guy!

Oh, I'm going to tear a strip out of him!, she thought as she released her vice like grip from the steering wheel, and pushed back her hair.

Her eyes widened in surprise as he got closer. *Sweet Lord,* she thought. *This guy looks like one of those underwear models you see on bus shelter poster ads. What are the odds of finding another black person out here?*

She found the wherewithal to roll down the window as he ran up to her driver's side door. His stunningly handsome face was only slightly marred by his expression of concern.

"What's an underwear model doing way out here?" she blurted. She put her hand to her mouth and she gasped at her own stupidity. "Was that my outside voice?"

He didn't seem to hear her, and said, "Are you all right? Are you hurt at all?" His voice was deep and husky. His light jacket emphasized his wide shoulders, and his jeans did little to hide his muscular thighs. For some bizarre reason his body reminded her of the trees all around, tall and strong.

Like a mountain man's!

"Yes," she finally managed to say. "I think I'm alive." She grinned up at him.

He sagged with relief, smiling for the first time, and she found his perfect teeth out did the brightness of the morning sun.

"Well, that's relief," he said, placing his hands on the rolled down window. She could not help but notice they were large and strong looking.

She caught herself wondering just how gentle those strong hands could be, moving up and down her body.

"I am so sorry," he said. "It was my fault. I didn't realize I was so close to the road. My car broke down." He hitched a thumb over at the little dodge parked on the road side.

"Oh, no, it was my fault," she said. "I wasn't paying attention, my thoughts drifted..." and as she said that she realized her drifting thoughts had been about a much needed man to distract her from her troubles. She looked up at his handsome face, with its chiseled features and strong jaw. *And I go ahead and nearly kill the only man for miles!*

"I can't get any reception on my phone," he said. "Could I use yours to call for a tow truck?"

"Sorry, but I don't have one," she said, sheepishly.

"Ah, that's too bad," he said, disappointed. He was looking at her, smiling, when she had a thunderous revelation.

"Hey," she said sweetly. "Since I almost splattered you all over the road, the least I could do is offer you a ride." She felt her face reddening as she spoke, trying not make it obvious what kind of ride she really had in mind.

He arched a brow, considering the offer. Finally, he said, "Where are you headed?"

"South. A long way south, actually."

He frowned a little and she was momentarily mortified she would lose him. But again, he regarded her with that sexy arch of the eyebrow. "I think the next town is only a couple of miles further up the road." He shrugged as if to suggest he really didn't want to bother her any more.

Oh, he could bother her, alright.

She grinned. "I'll take you. It's the least I could do. It might keep me from running you over again when I turn around."

He laughed. "Okay. You win. Just let me grab my stuff." He trotted back to his car.

She watched the movement of his buttocks in his jeans as he moved.

Yum, yum, yum, she thought.

She turned the car around in a wide arch, to point back in the southerly direction she was original travelling. This time she didn't almost kill him.

She watched as he grabbed a duffle bag from the front seat, then locked the car. Her heart was pounding excitedly in her chest. She looked at herself in the rear view mirror, and made a vain attempt at fixing her tussled hair. She locked eyes with herself.

Do you know what you are doing girl?

She grinned. *Yes, I'm going to be doing him!*

He came back, and threw his bag in the backseat. Then he sat down in the passenger side, closing the door. As he settled in, she sneaked a peak at his crotch.

Yup, she thought, *he definitely has a penis*. With that confirmed, she now had to find out if he knew how to use it.

He turned and smiled at her, offering his hand.

"I'm Bravon."

She took it, and tried not to shiver with the electric touch of him.

"Delonda."

They shook.

Delonda found she was unwilling to release is hand right away. But when he arched that brow again and added that cute smile, she relented. She pulled out on the road and drove, trying mightily to keep her eyes from staring at him.

They made very idle chit chat, of which none involved her getting naked, and him spanking her. She was just trying to work up the courage to make it happen. Yet, she got the distinct sense he was intrigued by her. Maybe even found her attractive.

It only took a few minutes but they arrived at the town turnoff. Her mind was racing. She had an impulse and by God she was going to see it through, this time! She slowed the car.

"Hey, what's that over there," she said pointing toward what looked like the entrance to an old dirt road that disappeared into the forest.

He looked. "Looks like a switchback road," he said. "Runaway truck use them in an emergency."

"Wow. I've never seen one of those maybe I'll go down a little ways just to check out. Would be nice and private." She looked at him meaningfully. "Care to come have an emergency with me?"

His eyebrows had raised in surprise making him look all the more adorable.

A second passed and then another, each feeling like years to Delonda.

He chuckled slightly, then settled back in his seat. He then regarded her with a seductive smile. "That's a fantastic idea," he said.

She laughed.

Hoping not to lose him in the moment, she quickly steered the car onto the switchback road.

She drove slowly down the gravel road while fully conscious of the glances he was giving her. The moment the highway seemed a safe distance out of view, she pulled over as far as she could and parked, again.

She turned the car off, and killed the power, too, and sat back.

They both grinned nervously at each other.

"Well," Delonda said. "What do we do now?"

Bravon made a show of looking around at their surroundings. "I dunno. Is this the spot you normally take the men you almost run over?"

She laughed, undid her seat belt, and moved over to him closing the distance. Placing a hand on his strong shoulder she whispered in his ear, "Yes, and I would like to suck your cock, as an apology." To ensure he did not miss her meaning, she grabbed the bulge in his jeans. She was happy to note that it was already growing in size.

"Yes, ma'am!" he said, and leaned back to undo his belt. She helped him. When it was undone he eased his hips forward so she would have room.

She fished his dick out of its hiding place, it was firm, big and erect. She kissed the tip several times, feeling its throbbing heat in her hand. Gently, she started to lick its length, up and down from the base of his shaft to the swollen prick. Like a lollipop.

He gasped softly, putting one hand on the back of her head to guide her up and down movements.

He then reached down, found the release for the chair and angled it back some more, giving her more room to work on him properly.

With his knob glistening from her diligent licking, she then took his fat prick into her mouth, pushing it up to the back of her throat as far as it would go. Her lips firmly gripped his shaft as they moved closer to the base, her nose touched his stomach. Then she sucked at it, moving her head up and down all the way. She stroked him with her hand, following it with her lips.

He groaned.

For several long wonderful minutes she sucked his cock, until he reached a point she was certain he was going to shoot his load. The car filled with sound of her hard sucking, and hungry slurping.

Carefully, she slowed, not wanting him to be spent too soon. Kissing the tip of his prick on more time, she then looked up at him with a big smile.

She said, “Let's fuck.”

He smiled back, but offered that cute arching brow again. “It's a little crowded in here for that, don't you think?”

She sat up a little and said, “Well, you are a big boy. Let's take this party outside.”

And with that they jumped out of the car. Before he moved around toward he she pointed at him and commanded, “Strip Mister!”

He laughed, but did as he was told, stripping his clothes off, his hard on quivering with each motion.

She did the same, deftly peeling off all her clothing in under a minute. They threw their clothes into the car. The gravel felt cool under her feet.

Bravon walked quickly around to her side of the car, holding his stiff dick.

“I want you to fuck me this way,” she said, motioning for him to get in back of her.

She stood standing with her arms braced, one against the open door, the other against the car roof. She spread her legs out a little and stuck her butt out, arching her back.

He smacked her ass, and moved up behind her. Holding his dick he rubbed its prick along the inside folds of her pussy, exploring her wetness, teasing her with it.

When she could no longer stand the anticipation commanded, “Fuck me! Just fuck me, dammit!”

“Okay,” he said, and suddenly lunged forward, jamming the entire length of him inside her with one motion.

She gasped, and gritted her teeth as he immediately started to pound against her. Her braced arms tensed with each impact. She delighted in knowing that if she hadn't held herself in such a way, he may very well of fucked her straight through the door with his powerful thrusts.

He pounded against her, over and over, until her moans grew louder and more intense. Her flesh grew red where he smashed up against her. He smacked her ass repeatedly, slapping each one in turn.

As he continued to fuck her, he licked his thumb and then rubbed it against her little ass-hole. He circled it with his thumb over and over.

Several minutes passed as he worked on her, and the forest filled with the sounds of their passionate efforts. She moaned, and occasionally yelped when he smacked her reddening flesh. He gasped, trying desperately not to cum just yet.

When he was close to being spent he slowed, easing in and out of her gently. He reached up and cupped her tits, which were perky and firm. He squeezed them, and pinched at her erect nipples.

Then, he pulled out of her, and smacked her ass loudly one more time.

"Ow!" she cried with delight.

"I want to eat your pussy," he said pointing toward the hood of the car.

She glowed. "Great idea!"

She giggled as she tiptoed to the front of the car. He followed in hot pursuit. The hood was sloped and she eased herself up it by wiggling her bum. Then she leaned back on her elbows and spread her legs.

The fibreglass popped and sagged with her weight.

"I don't think this car was designed for this," she said, not caring in the least.

"Let's see what else it wasn't designed for," he said with mischievous smile. He squatted in front of her, placing those strong hands against her widened thighs, then he leaned forward and gave her shaved pussy a nice long welcoming lick.

Then he licked again, and again, until he developed a rhythm. Delonda bent her head back and smiled gloriously up at the blue morning sky, enjoying the sensation of his tongue all over her pussy.

Eventually, he sucked on one of his fingers to get it wet, then he cautiously slipped it up inside her, and she gasped. Then he started to make a come-hither motion against the sensitive pad just behind her pubic bone. She shivered with pleasure, practically seeing stars before her eyes with the intensity.

He returned to work, concentrating more now on her clit. He sucked at it, tickling it with his tongue at the same time. All the while, she gasped with pleasure, squeezing her tits, pinching at their erect nipples. She took one in her mouth and teethed it, sucking.

He ate her out for long moments, listening to the wet sounds his gyrating finger made inside her.

When he had his fill he then stood, cock hard and ready. He leaned forward, so he was hovering over her, and bent his dick as far as it would go. He stuck his prick into her waiting pussy. She gasped, and grabbed onto his hips.

"You want this?" he asked.

"Yes!" she begged. "Fuck the hell outta me!"

And with that, he suddenly slammed the entire length of his long dick deep inside her. She gasped with the hard penetration. He then lifted his ass up again, so his entire dick was nearly unsheathed from her, and slammed it down again.

The hood of the car popped and squawked with the hard pressured movements.

Over and over he did this, getting faster and faster. She moaned with each pelvic thrust. Long wonderful minutes passed as he slammed her pussy again and again. Eventually, the intensity got to be so much Delonda's eyes rolled upwards, completely lost in the rapture of the moment.

Over and over; again and again he slammed down onto her.

He could not keep up the relentless pace. With both the feeling of the rubbing wet friction inside her, and seeing her face grimace with the concentrated effort of their passion, he found himself about to orgasm.

"I'm gonna cum!" he finally shouted.

Quickly, Delonda pushed him back, unsheathing him form her.

He stood before her, stroking his cock vigorously. Sitting on the edge of the hood, she leaned forward so she could place the bottom of her open mouth against the base of his prick. Her tongue tickled at it eagerly, and her eyes stared up at him with hunger.

He stroked faster, and soon came with a loud moan. His semen spat out all over her; hot squirts into her mouth which slid down her tongue and pooled at the back of her throat. Over her face in long sticky strands that splayed across her cheeks and forehead. In the corner of one eye, down her chin, and he even got some in her hair.

As he sagged with completion, she made a dramatic show of swallowing.

She smacked her mouth, and rolled her tongue around her lips, getting every white bit. A long thick strand still hung from her chin as she grinned widely at him.

She then grabbed his dick, and sucked it as his erection faded, nursing the last of his load.

Looking up at his handsome face, seeing the sunshine glint off the sweat on his muscular chest, she came to a conclusion:

She needed to almost run over hunks more often!

END

Criminal Seduction

"Committing crime gets me seriously wet," Chanara said. "So what are you gonna do about it?"

Shotgun in one hand, a box of bullets in the other, Kadaris paused. He looked at Chanara who had just came out of the shower wrapped in a towel. She flopped onto the squeaky hotel bed, dark wet hair sticking to her bare shoulders.

"Can't, babe," he said. "No time. You know that don't you?" He sat on the corner of the bed and started to load rounds into the shotgun. Each one done with a methodical sense of purpose.

Chanara managed a pout, sliding one hand up under the back of his shirt. His flesh was wonderfully warm to the touch; hard and muscular. "We have a little extra time. The manager always arrives at the same exact time. We've seen him."

Kadaris tried to focus on his task but found it difficult as her caress stoked his inner flame. Hitting this particular bank had been Chanara's idea. He could tell she was excited about it and needed to let some of that out. He pretended to consider her request. "I dunno," he said.

She smiled. He caved to her desires so easily. She watched for a few moments as he loaded the weapon.

His muscular forearms seriously turned her on. Both with sleeved tattoos right down to the wrists. Images of coiled serpents, pillars of colourful fire and leering demonic skulls. She could gaze at them all day.

Better yet, she preferred if they were wrapped around her all day. Holding her close. "You like that gun more than me?" she teased.

"Never," he said. "But to keep us flush with cash we need to focus on the job." He offered her a commiserating smile. "After we're finished, babe. I promise."

Kadaris loaded the last shell and stood, pulling away from her. It made her unhappy. "I'll give you something to point that at," Chanara said.

With that she pushed herself to a kneeling on the bed, and slowly removed the towel. With a flourish, she cast the towel away.

His eyes took her in. Her incredible form, still glowing slightly from the shower, beckoned to him even more so than any bank vault could.

A detailed tattoo of a black panther was on one shoulder; it's feline form extended down the supple slope of her breast, its jaws opened, as if ready to bite the perky nipple.

Smiling, she put her hands on her hips, the motion causing her ample tits to jiggle pleasantly. "Care for some pre-robbery fun?"

Damn! He thought. *What a fine piece of ass!*

Kadaris jammed the last round into the shotgun. "Hell, yeah. Why not? We can make time."

He was about to put the shotgun down onto the nightstand when Chanara motioned for him not to.

"No, I wanna do something," she said.

"What?"

"Something different." Chanara laid on her back, her knees pointed toward Kadaris. With a wicked grin she open her legs, the angle of her muscular thighs made is crotch ache.

Exposed to him in all its beautiful, wet glory was her pussy.

Curious, he asked, "What did you have in mind, girl?"

She grinned. "Got a holster for that gun of yours, mister."

Kadaris was perplexed. "Shotguns don't need holsters." He held it up giving it a comical look of confusion.

Chanara giggled. "That one does." Her hands moved down her belly, past the small triangle thatch of pubic hair, and down to her pussy. She spread her pussy lips with her fingers, exposing the wet pink within. "Right here," she said.

Kadaris laughed. "Think it's to big." He arched an eyebrow at her. "Won't fit."

"Then that's your problem," she said. She started to gently play with her clit as she looked up at him with hooded eyes. "You have experience jamming big things into tight, wet spaces."

Kadaris' eyes went wide. "God. You are a wild one, aren't you, babe?" He put one knee up on the mattress so he was between her open legs, her feet hooking around his waist.

"You know it," she said.

He eased the shotgun forward finding himself getting aroused with the image of the shotgun between beautiful naked legs, and inches away from her hot pussy.

Chanara grabbed at the shotgun with both hands. For a moment Kadaris thought she was going to thrust it inside her. Instead, she started to slowly run her hands up and down the barrel. She jerked the shotgun like this for long moments, pretending it was his cock.

Gradually she jerked at it faster and faster. One hand cupped and explored the barrel opening, her fingers probing inside.

She gave him a half smile. “Don't blow your load just yet.” She placed one foot on his wide shoulder. Toyed his ear with her toes.

Kadaris was positively salivating at that point. He wanted to cast the shotgun aside and fuck her right then and there.

As if sensing his intentions, Chanara stopped masturbating the long barrel and slowly drew it closer to her.

As if hypnotized Kadaris could only watch.

She gently ran the edge of the barrel up the length of her pussy. The soft wet lips parted slightly to this intrusion. When she reached her clit, she circled the barrel around it. First clockwise for several slow strokes, then the other way. Her head pushed back against the mattress, succulent tits quivering. Her nipples her hard and incredibly erect.

Then she slowly ran the barrel edge down her pussy, this time pressing against her flesh a little harder. Again, her lips parted, but exposed more.

Kadaris could see pussy juice sticking to the barrel. He wanted very much to suck it all up, but resisted. He concentrated on holding the gun steady and enjoyed the show.

There barrel seemed to catch at the wider bottom edge of her wet cunt, but Chanara continued downward. She angled her legs back until her ankles were up near her own ears. Her little dark asshole presented itself to Kadaris. It puckered slightly, as if winking at him.

Flexible girl, Kadaris thought.

She then firmly pressed the double barrels against her bare taint. When she removed it he could see the indelible impression of the double barrel openings in her skin, like a figure eight.

Further down she moved it.

Kadaris started to sweat. The shotgun quivered a little in his grasp.

"Don't lose your cool now, big boy," Chanara breathed.

Kadaris strengthened his resolve. The gun stopped shaking.

Past the taint, Chanara eased the barrel edge over her asshole. Its exploration continuing over this lustful landscape.

She circled her asshole with it, over and over. Occasionally, she would flex her anus, open and closed, with ever complete circle. Her breathing was getting heavier.

Unable to help himself, Kadaris guided the barrel until it was directly on the opening.

Chanara smiled. "Spit!" she commanded.

Happy to oblige, Kadaris leaned forward over the gun barrel until his nose touched the bottom fleshy part of her pussy. With his mouth, he slowly let out a long gob of saliva. It landed on the gun barrel and slide down over Chanara's asshole. Unsatisfied, he spit some more. He used the barrel to spread the spit around her anus until it gleamed in the hotel room's ruddy lighting.

"Now stick it in," Chanara whispered.

Slowly, with almost glacial like movements, Kadaris helped her push the barrel edge into her ass. At first it seemed to resist the foreign object outright, but Kadaris knew Chanara loved anal sex, and he had loosened her up that way on many occasions.

With some gentle prodding the edge of the barrel slipped in. Her anus clasped its smooth metal almost hungrily.

Kadaris chuckled. "Fuck yeah!" This was impressive. Chanara always could get her freak on.

With the help of his spit, the barrel slide into her. Just a few centimetres. Then he pulled it back, but not enough to pop out. Then back in again. The firm grasp of her asshole clung to the barrel almost possessively.

Several times they did this. Then, almost without warning, Chanara pushed the barrel further inside her, several inches. She paused. Kadaris was beside himself with amazement. Her was this little sex goddess, naked in front of him, with a gun stuffed her bung hole.

"I am one lucky fucker," he said aloud.

Chanara didn't respond. Her concentration was on getting the barrel further into her pliable flesh. In and out she moved it. Long lengths it slid. Her asshole now fully accepting the barrel's form; enveloping it completely with its movements.

Lost in concentration, Kadaris didn't hear Chanara speak to him. He shook his head, snapping out of his trance. "Sorry, babe. What was that?"

"I said stick it in my cunt. I know that will make me cum." She smiled at him. "You want me to cum don't you?"

Kadaris grinned. "Damn straight." Gently, he pulled the barrel out of her ass. Her asshole made a wet farting noise as the barrel popped out. They both giggled.

He aimed at her pussy, which seemed to glow wetly with anticipation. Slowly, he moved it closer.

Suddenly, Chanara grabbed the barrel. "No need to be so careful. You know my cunt can take the abuse!" And with that, she yanked on the gun, almost pulling it out of Kadaris' hands.

Instantly, she jammed a good six inches of the steel barrel into herself. Kadaris helped, enjoying himself immensely. He worked the barrel back and forth, using more of the barrel length than he had done with her asshole.

Soon, he was sliding in and out over 10 inches of length. The metal was slick with her cunt juice.

Chanara moaned, arching her back. She had let go of the barrel and gripped the bedsheets with intensity.

More and more Kadaris fucked her with the shotgun, in and out over and over. Chanara's whole body now gyrated and shook with the rapturous act. Her pussy was making wet farting noises with every thrust and pull.

"Faster!" she cried.

"I am!" he said. And he was. So much so his arms were starting to get tired. He almost felt like a plumber trying to unclog a particularly difficult drain.

Then, Chanara gasped with near ecstasy.

"You okay, babe?" Kadaris asked.

She seemed to be trying to catch her breath. Kadaris grew concerned.

"Want me to stop?"

"Nooooooo!" she shouted at the ceiling. She started to finger her clit almost angrily.

"What?"

"Rack it!" she cried.

"What?"

"The shotgun! Rack a round into it! Now!"

Kadaris obliged, although he was careful to make sure the safety was still on, and his finger was no where near the trigger. Hey, this was her kink, and he was happy to play along. Just didn't need to accidentally shoot her head off through her cunt.

The dark humour made him grin wider, and he racked a round into the chamber, keeping the barrel buried deep inside her hungry wet cunt. The shotgun made a loud CHUCK-CHUCK noise.

That movement sent Chanara over the edge as she furiously fingered her exposed clit. She bucked, and moaned wildly.

Kadaris loved every second of it. "Fuck yeah, babe!" he said.

Her orgasm fading, Chanara reached down and grabbed the shotgun barrel. She guided in and out of herself, letting the feeling ease her arousal. Finally, after several long moments Kadaris slid it out of her.

She gasped with pleasure, pinching her tits. The flesh around her pussy was sopping wet, and the flesh of her cunt was spread wide and a bright pink. Kadaris bent down and gave her pussy a long sloppy kiss, slurping up some of its succulent juice.

"You're a wild child," he said, chin wet.

Still squeezing her tits and rubbing at her nipples she said, "You make me wild."

Kadaris looked at the end of the shotgun barrel. It gleamed with her wetness. "I'm normally anal about keeping my guns clean since they're the main tool of our trade. But I'm not gonna this time. If I gotta pull the trigger on someone we'll think of it as pussy shots."

This made Chanara howl with laughter. *Fuck, Kadaris was hot!* She thought to herself.

She crawled over to him and began to wrestle with his belt. The bulge in his jeans was prominent to the point of bursting through the fabric.

Kadaris gently took her hands, stopping her. She pouted.

"I wanna suck you off, babe," she said, licking her lips with blatant hunger. "Suck your real barrel off until there isn't a drop left." She sounded almost like a crazed animal.

Kadaris was about to agree when the alarm on his phone went off. "Shit," he said. "No time now. Got to keep on schedule." He gently pushed her away.

She agreed, but could not mask her disappointment. They were professionals after all. But even professionals could be allowed to have some fun.

Kadaris put his game face on, suddenly serious. "Let's get going. We have an appointment with riches we can't miss."

Chanara quickly dressed as Kadaris double checked their gear. She loved watching him when he was like this. Together, they were bad. Really really bad. And now they were going to do something that would prove to the world how bad they could be.

They carried their gear in tout bags out of their hotel room. People passed them by not realizing what was inside them. This gave Chanara a secret thrill.

As they walked toward Kadaris' Mustang he could not help but notice Chanara was walking with a slight limp.

"Feeling a little sore this morning, miss?" He said with a knowing smile.

Chanara's smile matched his. "Yeah. Feel like a just got reamed raw by a shotgun. You'd limp, too."

Kadaris laughed. "Don't go getting any more ideas now in that pretty head of yours."

She stuck her tongue out at him.

They threw the touts into the back seat and climbed into the front. Almost in unison they put sunglasses on.

"Couple of bad asses," Kadaris said.

Chanara checked the time. "Hey! We're way ahead of schedule." She glared at him, thinking of how much more gun play she could have had back in the room.

"Know why?" Kadaris asked as he started the Mustang. The engine rumbled to life like a living beast.

"Why?"

Kadaris put it in drive. "Cause we're fucking professionals. That's why." He slammed on the gas. The Mustang surged forward across the parking lot. He peeled out onto the road.

They both laughed at the reactions of the people how gaped at them. Charged up with sex and an impending crime, they were ecstatic.

The hotel was only ten minutes distance from the bank, and Kadaris got them there in three minutes. Soon, they turned onto the block with the bank up on the left hand side.

Chanara's heart was now pounding with excitement. Other than getting fucked by Kadaris, nothing else was as thrilling as hitting a bank. They had done enough of them to settle on a comfortable, and safe routine.

Casually as can be, they drove past the bank. While Kadaris watched the road, playing the dutiful driver, Chanara looked.

"Anything unusual?" he said as he turned down a side street. They would loop around to their waiting spot.

"Nothing," she said. "No one inside yet."

"Perfect," Kadaris said.

"No, you're perfect," she said, smiling.

"We're perfect little devils," he said as he smoothly pulled into a spot on the side of the road. From here they had the perfect vantage point of the front door, as well as anything along the side of the bank building. Just as they originally planned.

Now they just had to sit and wait.

The street was quiet, with only the occasional passerby in the distance.

Chanara gave Kadaris a serious look. "You didn't let me suck you off back at the hotel."

"No time."

She motioned to the bank. "We got time. You promised I could have it. Why not a little fun while we wait."

Before Kadaris could tell her no she said, "I'll stop as soon as he comes. Or you cum. Whoever *cums* first." She offered him a most enticing smile.

Kadaris tried to argue the point but knew her hunger for his cock was insatiable. Besides, it *would* help ratchet down the tension he was feeling.

Chanara took his hesitation as a yes. She squealed with joy and shifter over to him in the seat. She fumbled with his belt buckle. "Got to let the beast out of its cage. Poor thing."

Kadaris eased the driver's seat back a little as Chanara undid his belt and then his zipper. They both gave a quick look around. No one. Perfect.

She dug into his open pants and fished for his cock which flopped out. He was already partially erect.

"Fuck yeah," Chanara said. She leaned in close to it. Kadaris could feel her breath on his prick, her long dark hair caressing his exposed skin.

She started jerking at it. Turning her head to look up at him she said, "No time for foreplay, honey. Gonna make this quick but sweet."

"Yeah," Kadaris said. He could feel his dick getting harder. Still, he managed to keep one eye on the front of the bank.

Chanara eased up a little on the tugging action, and slowly spit on his prick. Not satisfied there was enough she spit even more. The top of his cock was covered in her saliva, with one string of spittle extending from her bottom lip to the side of his shaft.

Like the fluttering wings of a butterfly, she flickered her tongue against his wet swollen prick. Several times she spit again, and even kissed the top of its head with pouted lips. She enjoyed the noise she made when she kissed his dick.

Suddenly, a man walked by their car.

Kadaris, alarmed, grabbed the back of her head with one hand. Thinking he wanted her to swallow his cock, Chanara bent her head down, engulfing the entire length of his sizable dick with one motion.

Kadaris gasped, tensing up. The man had sauntered by without even looking in their direction. He turned a corner and was gone.

Chanara gagged on his dick. She had plunged it so its prick was now firmly lodged inside her throat several inches. But she was a trooper and held her head there. Her nose was jammed into the warm flesh of his left pelvis, and her lips were against the skin at the very base of his shaft.

The small trim forest of his pubic hair tickled her face. His testicles were now touching her right cheek.

Her mouth was *crammed* full, yet with amazing skill honed over the years of sucking many, many dicks, she managed to play her tongue around the ample shaft.

"Shiiiiiiit," Kadaris moaned.

Chanara held herself there, feeling his throbbing cock deep inside her throat, and practically pushing against the back of her skull. She breathed through her nose, Kadaris' pubic hair tickle her nostrils.

Then, after several long minutes, she slowly moved up his cock, slurping noisily the whole time.

She withdrew his dick, coughing and sputtering a little. His cock was absolutely slick with her spit, its prick glistening pleasantly in the morning sun.

Taking a few quick breathes, she then jammed it back into her mouth and up into her throat again. Then she withdrew. She did this over and over. Cock all in, cock all out.

Soon, she started to pick up speed. With a little adjustments to her technique she was in full suck mode.

Kadaris was going practically cross eyed, holding the back of her head with one hand, the other on the steering wheel. He was mindful to not go near the car horn.

He really started to get into it as he felt the phantom tickle of an impending orgasm draw near. He grabbed her head with both hands and started to gyrate his hips while in his seat. His cock moved up and down into Chanara's welcoming hot mouth.

Faster and faster he thrust into her skull, like a piston on a race car about to blow out. Deep into her throat, he thrust. Chanara could feel his prick pummelling the back of it.

And she loved it.

The car was filled with the rapid sound of Chanara's wet continuous suction.

Then, it happened. Kadaris moaned in pleasure, his body going tense.

From within her throat, Chanara felt his hot seed shoot into it. Kadaris had stopped fucking her face as he came. She got a firm grip on his shaft and kept sucking. Her lips never lost their wet grip on his cock, ensuring every last sticky drop of his hot cum went right were it belonging. In her mouth.

Kadaris let out another rapturous moan. Chanara had now managed to literally suck him dry. No more cum to suck out of him.

Suddenly, Kadaris sat upright.

"Shit!" Kadaris hissed.

"What?"

"The bank manager. He's here!"

From his lap, Chanara peered out the front windshield. "Oh, crap. He's early. Way early." She looked at Kadaris. "Does this mess things up? Can we still do it?" She sat up, wiping cum from her lips and licking them quickly.

Kadaris put his wet dick back into his pants and did up his zipper. He offered his trademark evil-doers grin. "Honey," he said. "We can do *anything*."

They watched as the manager unlocked the door, oblivious to anyone who might be watching. Chanara made sure her face was clean of jizz in the side view mirror. She coughed up a little burp, the kind given after a good meal.

Kadaris chuckled. "Like a pig in a poke."

A couple of women, bank tellers arrived, too. The manager let them in, and followed after.

Chanara was eager. "Did he leave the door unlocked again?"

"Yup," said Kadaris. "Just like every morning for the last two weeks."

Chanara laughed.

"Let's do this," Kadaris said. They leaned into each other and kissed passionately. Their tongues seeking each other out with a wild hunger.

Then they got out of the Mustang, and grabbed their bags. From those they took out a pair of long coats and put them on. Then, with a quick glance around to see if there was no one else looking, they withdrew their shotguns, and hide them under their coats.

They walked purposefully towards the bank door. Looking up and down the street, checking again, they then withdrew full masks. Devil's Heads masks, complete with little horns. His was red, hers was blue.

"Don't need these masks to know how bad we are, baby." Kadaris said as he pulled his on.

When Chanara did the same, they nodded at each other and went inside.

Chanara locked the door behind them.

Kadaris was already striding across the bank which, because they planned it that way, was empty of customers. The tellers were over at a coffee machine, contemplating its slow percolation.

"Down on the floor, NOW!" he shouted.

The tellers looked at him in shock. The manager came running out of his office, a half eaten doughnut in his hand.

Kadaris fired into the ceiling. The noise was deafening. "I said now!"

All three of them dropped to the ground.

Chanara had taken several steps into the bank to cover him, but her main job was to watch for other employees arriving. She would drag them in until the job was finished.

That was to be her focus. This was a serious situation after all.

Yet, standing there with his shotgun pointed at the tellers Chanara could not help but marvel at Kadaris.

Up on the teller's counter, screaming hellfire at anyone who didn't move quick enough, he looked absolutely gorgeous. A sleek, well defined, tattooed god.

And just a few minutes earlier, her mouth was full of his fat cock, his cum spilling down her throat. She grinned.

Kadaris threw an empty tout bag at the manager. "Fill it! Fast!"

The manager hasten to do as he was told. Chanara could see him stuffing huge handfuls of cash into the bag from the tellers counter.

Money! Money! Money!

Kadaris made one of the tellers fill another bag.

He looked over at Chanara who checked outside for the thirtieth time, then nodded at him.

Kadaris grabbed the full bag from the manager and told him to get on the ground. Then he did the same with teller.

He backed up towards Chanara, all the while watching the others cowering on the floor. He passed a bag over to Chanara. Its weight was orgasmic!

"Stay down, or we'll come back and massacre you all!" He shouted with menace.

Chanara unlocked the door and stepped outside. Kadaris followed. Amazingly, the street was quiet. Still too early. Luck was on there side.

They hustled toward the Mustang. They didn't want it in front of the bank in case it created a drama for being parked there.

Chanara was absolutely charged up. "We did it!"

Kadaris was all business. "Not yet. We still gotta..."

Just then they heard sirens. Lots of them. And close by.

"Oh, shit!" he said. "Move!"

They ran to the Mustang, threw the full bags in the backseat, and quickly got inside. Chanara hung onto her shotgun, eyes scanning around.

Kadaris started the car with a loud revving, and they quickly sped off.

About three blocks away Chanara looked back. As Kadaris turned a corner she caught the glimpse of a black and white cop car, lights flashing, sirens blaring, race past. It was headed towards the bank.

She let out a relieved sigh. "They're not following us."

Kadaris was concentrating on the road. "Not yet. They will be soon enough if we don't get to the warehouse now."

Once they were a further distance away from the bank and the noise of sirens, Kadaris slowed down a little so as not to be pulled over for speeding.

Soon, they were in the warehouse district. They had scouted this place out beforehand, thoroughly, and knew exactly where to go. Into an abandoned section was a run down and empty warehouse building.

Kadaris pulled up to its loading dock door. Chanara got out. While she rolled the door up, Kadaris drove the Mustang around, and skillfully backed in through the door. Chanara pulled the door down.

He parked the Mustang in the middle the wide empty warehouse. The engine noise echoing throughout. He killed it and got out. Chanara ran over to him.

"We did it, babe!" she shouted as she leaped into his arms for a big hug.

They kissed passionately, tongues going deep into the other's mouth.

"Now what?" she asked.

"Now we stick to the plan. We wait."

She pouted at him, playing it up. "That's gonna be a while. Hiding out here until things cool down." She pressed her hand up against his crotch. "While things cool down out there, they can heat up in here. Got to pass the time somehow."

Kadaris laughed. "Okay, babe. You convinced me." He knew they would not be bothered here and could hideout here for days if necessary.

Delighted, Chanara stepped back from him and peeled off her shirt. Her wonderful breasts popped out enticingly. Then went the pants and panties. Soon she was buck naked in front of him, her tattoo prominent across her breast.

"You next," she demanded.

Kadaris obliged, and quickly followed suite. He felt a little silly standing naked in the cool empty warehouse, cock in his hand.

"Well, we got time," he looked at her meaningfully. "So lets make it count. Where you want to do it? On the hood? In the back seat?" He smiled. "On the roof?"

She shook her head. "Nope. I got a better idea. Something we've never done before."

Naked, tits jiggling, she walked over to the Mustang, Chanara leaned into it and pulled out one of the tout bags. She grinned wickedly at him. Then, she upturned the bag, and wads of cash spilt out onto the concrete floor.

"What are you doing?" Kadaris said, incredulous.

Chanara reached into the Mustang again. This time she pulled out a shotgun. She pointed it at him.

Eyes wide, cautioning hands in the air, Kadaris said, "Babe? What the hell?"

She gave him a serious look now. "I want to fuck on a bed of money!" She racked a round into the shotgun. CHUCK-CHUCK! "Now get you bare ass down on the ground. I'm gonna ride you long and hard!"

Kadaris chuckled. *Fuckin Wild Child!*

Still naked, he did as he was told. He lay down on the cold floor, cash in their bank wrappers pressing against his skin.

Chanara smiled and sauntered over, her beautiful naked form was actually made all the more sexier by the shotgun in her hands. She spread her legs on either side of him as she moved forward until she stood over his crotch.

Her hot pussy presented itself to him. For a moment, Kadaris was happily overwhelmed but the dominance she had over him.

Slowly, Chanara squatted down, shotgun in both hands pointed at the ceiling.

For a moment they heard the faint sound of a distant siren. They both paused. It faded away. She smiled back down at him. Squatting over him, she slide her pussy back and forth against the length of his penis.

"Put it in me," she commanded.

Kadaris used a hand and pointed his fat dick upwards. Chanara eased down on it, until she enveloped him completely. Slowly she rocked her hips forward and back, all the while still holding the shotgun. She was incredibly wet. Turned on by the crime they just committed. Turned on by the pursuing cops.

Turned on by *him.*

Faster and faster she gyrated, perfect tits jiggling, the shotgun pressed against them. Occasionally she bounced up and down, the wet smacking noise of their flesh hitting each other filling the empty warehouse.

Again, there was the faint sound of sirens, but neither one of the them gave it any notice.

Kadaris played with her tits, squeezing them, pinching her nipples. She moved the shotgun away from herself slightly so he could do so. She looked down on him with hooded eyes.

Soon in became to much for Kadaris; her succulent body grinding his cock, bouncing on him. The movement of her tits. Her excited breathing. The robbery. The sound of sirens.

Chanara did not let up, grinding with full force against him, feeling his dick flop around insider her. She actually growled with the intensity.

Kadaris came. He bucked wildly, hands digging into her hips harder as she still moved against him. Soon he was completely spent. He gasped with pleasure.

"Fuuuuuuck...." he said. He had a goofy grin plastered on his face.

Chanara leaned down and kissed him, sweaty tits pressing against his sweaty chest.

"Know what, baby?" Chanara said.

"No, tell me. I like to be informed." Kadaris was starting to feel a little exhausted from the day's activities.

"Post-robbery sex is the *best*!" Chanara declared.

They laughed.

END

Had she known that incredible sex would be the result of a job interview, Brayonna would have applied for it a lot sooner.

She found the position at a major marketing firm as an sales associate, doing mundane sales calls. It was a job, nothing more nothing less. Certainly not a career for her by any stretch, but it paid her rent and bills, allowing her to save a little for more a new car.

Of course, she had no idea that when she took it that she would be seeing naked people at work, doing delightfully naked things together. Perhaps she should really be considering this factor as a bonus.

In hindsight, her interview did have clues. She had found the job posting online, and emailed her resume with cover letter. Her experience was water thin, having only just graduated from college. Throngs of other sales associates with much more mileage than her, had no doubt applied as well. Yet, the very next day, she got a phone call from Oday, the manager, and, yes, the manager who would later show he could not keep it in his pants.

At first, Brayonna was excited to be speaking to him. Any call from an employer was a good call in her books. He had asked some general questions about her schooling, then arranged for an interview.

She was thrilled to the point of being ecstatic. It hadn't occurred to her right then that something might be a little amiss, or to wonder why she of all people would be asked for further questioning for a job she was sorely under qualified for. At best, she had hoped for an entry level position. She was certainly more than capable to do the posted job, but her expectations of getting it were low.

Arriving fifteen minutes early - she always showed up early for everything, even her best friend, Sherri, had said she would even be early for her own funeral - and waited in the plush office lobby. She was a little intimidated with the fancy surroundings. This was obviously a company with cash to spend, and were not afraid to use it to impress.

That was a good sign, or so she thought.

The receptionist was amazingly cute. Tall, statuesque beauty who was exceedingly cheerful. The dress she wore certainly showed off her figure, and made Brayonna envious.

She idly wondered how the brunette would look like without that dress. But before she could venture forth with that wonderfully imaginative scenario, Oday's assistant arrived and showed her in.

Cabrina was her name, and as she guided Brayonna through the maze of cubicles she told her she had been working for Oday for almost two years and liked it. Brayonna sneaked glances at her body. Dark, curvy and with an ample bosom that bounced firmly as she walked. Brayonna made a tremendous effort not to drool, or let another wonderful scenario distract her from the situation at hand.

Arriving at a corner office, Cabrina introduced her to Oday. Brayonna was actually a little taken aback.

He was gorgeous. Tall, dark, handsome. Chiseled jaw, and sparkling brown eyes, and a very athletic body.

Bonus! she had thought to herself as they shook hands. She found his touch to be electrifying. *So many other beautiful, sexy black people here.*

After exchanging initial pleasantries, he motioned for her to sit. The furnishings in his office was quit high end, even having a nice leather couch with twin chairs.

He indicated one of these, and she sat, while he did the same in the other, kitty corner to hers. She actually like the fact he wanted to talk there, as opposed to at his desk, which would have felt more formal and intimidating.

As Cabrina stepped out, Brayonna actually thought she caught her exchange a knowing smile with Oday. Or maybe it was her imagination. When the door closed Oday turned his attention, and that very handsome visage, to her.

"Thank you for coming," he had said, showing some very healthy white teeth.

Maybe that was a good indication of the dental benefits here, she had mused to herself.

"Of course, thank you for calling me in," she said.

They chatted, and his questions were more a furtherance of their phone call. But as they talked, she noticed his eyes would occasionally flicker to her legs (she was wearing a long skirt), or her bosom (no cleavage, thank you, she was professional after all). She took this in stride. She was more than use to men checking out her goods, even in a professional environment. These things happened. It was hard to keep the man and woman aspects completely aside, after all.

And besides, she felt she was more than worth checking out.

I'm a babe, and he knows it, she had thought to herself, as she spoke to him about system software. *And he's a babe, too.*

She found her eyes flickering occasionally during strategic moments when he glanced away, at his various manly parts. She wasn't sure if he noticed or not, and if she was to be completely honest with herself, she didn't really care.

When they reached the end of the conversation, he went quiet for a moment, as if thinking. She wondered if that thinking involved her being naked, and him on top of her. Maybe even on his desk over there.

She tried to keep her focus on the moment.

Finally, as if reaching a decision he said, "Well, I'm impressed. Can you start on Monday?"

Brayonna was stunned, to say the least. He was giving her the job? Her mouth hung open in surprise.

He chuckled at her expression, and said, "You are available aren't you?" There was slight playful teasing tone to his deep voice.

"Um, yes," she finally blurted out. "Yes, I am!" This had all happened way too fast for her brain to compute. Not only did she not expect a call back of any kind from her emailed resume, she certainly did not think she had a faint hope of a chance of actually getting the job.

She was ecstatic! But she did her best to contain herself and present a professional manner.

Again, he offered another big smile. "That's great. I'll get Cabrina to arrange things for you so you can start without a hitch." They stood, and walked to the door.

Brayonna wanted to do cartwheels across his office, but instead walked with her head held high.

When Oday told Cabrina, his assistant beamed, "Oh, that's wonderful! I'll make sure everything is set up for you when you arrive first thing Monday." Cabrina's eyes seemed to twinkle, and, this time, Brayonna was certain the other woman's eyes glanced down at her bosom.

I guess they both want to check out the goods they just bought, she thought to herself, not in the least bit put off by this. She was actually flattered.

Brayonna said she could see herself out, "May as well start getting to know my way around they place," she had said to their laughter. As she walked away, she happened to glance back at them.

Both Cabrina and Oday were standing side by side, very close together, watching her. They were both smiling brightly, and their expression reminded her of hungry kids looking throw the window of a candy store.

That weekend, her mind continued to see them smiling at her, and she realized that they had also been checking out her bum, as she walked away. Brayonna knew her bum was most certainly worthy of checking out. And, it was only fair, after all, she had checked out theirs, too.

She started Monday, and things got interesting right away.

Cabrina had given her a tour to help her acclimatize to her new office surroundings. The rest of the office and work areas were lavish, and it reminded her of big lawyer offices you see in the movies.

Back at her desk she started to familiarize herself with her new job. After several hours she realized she needed to pull some files, and her coworker, Leeda, who directly next to her, gave her a pass key for the secure filing room at the back of at the other side of the building.

The back filing office was huge. High shelves stuffed with big binders, and towering filing cabinets, made a little maze that she found confusing. She started the hunt for what she needed.

Then she heard a noise. She had thought she was alone back here, but the confusing layout obviously hid someone else who no doubt was hunting, too. Unable to find what she was looking for she hoped that perhaps they could assist her in her search.

"Hello?" she said. No one responded, but she heard the noise again. A bumping sound. She wend her way through the narrow alleyways of filing, trying to locate the source.

As she got closer, the bumping sound become more clearer. It was like a washing machine had been overloaded and was bashing against a wall.

Then she heard a gasp, and muffled voices.

They weren't really saying anything, more like they were moaning.

Intrigued, despite herself, she peeked around the corner of a cabinet, and that's when she saw them.

In the far flung corner of the room, way out of sight of the filing room's only door, was a man and woman. And there were doing some filing, all right, just not the kind this area was designated for.

The man's back was to Brayonna, and his dress pants and boxer shorts were pulled down to his knees. His dress shirt was hiked up, exposing smooth muscular buttocks that were clenching as he moved it back and forth.

A woman had her legs wrapped around him; she was perched on a stack of boxes which wobbled and shifted with their shared movement. Her skirt was synched up around her waist, and her hips were angled so better to receive him. She had her arms around his thick neck, and her eyes were closed in pleasurable ecstasy.

Brayonna recognized her instantly. It was Cabrina!

As he pumped her hard, the man turned his head slightly so as to suck on Cabrina's ear. It was Oday!

Brayonna was paralysed with shock, having just stumbled upon people having sex in the back of the office. And not just any people either, but her manager and his assistant.

Yet, she did not shy away, nor say anything to disturb them. She actually was starting to enjoy this little show.

They had obviously been going at it for a while; they were both breathing heavy, and glazed with sweat. Cabrina arched her back as Oday continued to pound her, almost relentlessly. She moaned, and made an obvious effort to keep it subdued.

For several minutes Brayonna watched the two lovers. She started to feel immensely guilty but shrugged it off. If they were going to do it right here in the office, where any could stumble upon them, then she was gonna watch!

Perhaps it was the thrill of possibly being discovered that lead them to take this risk. They could lose their jobs over this. This made Brayonna smile inwardly.

Now that was an interesting piece of information. Was she evil enough to take advantage of this little situation that has presented itself? Possibly. But, then again, who's to say they wouldn't find a reason to fire her if they suspected she knew?

She really needed this job, and was willing to do anything to keep it.

Just then, Oday pulled out of Cabrina, and stepped back. For a brief moment Brayonna saw Cabrina's pussy, wet and raw from being slammed so hard. It looked very appetizing, and she envisioned herself licking it all over.

She would even lick Oday's cum out of that pussy, too.

Shuddering at the prospect she watched as Cabrina deftly jumped off the boxes and fell to her knees in front of Oday. Her ample butt jiggled, and Brayonna could see she had the tan line from wearing a thong bikini.

Oday was stroking his dick, grinding his teeth trying to keep from cumming too soon. Cabrina grabbed it, and leaned forward, taking it all in her mouth. She sucked hard and fast. She seemed desperate to make him finish. The wet slurping noise she made filled the filing room.

Brayonna was starting to get hot, watching her work. She wanted to be sucking Oday off, too. She was almost tempted to reveal herself and join in, whether they wanted her or not. But she refrained. Instead, she grabbed at her on breasts, squeezing them through her dress and bra. She had particularly sensitive nipples, and was able to enjoy the sensation.

Just then, Oday moaned and grabbed at Cabrina's head. She sucked none stop, never letting up. Oday bucked, his hips and butt moving with spasms as he fucked her mouth and came inside it.

Cabrina chuckled while her sucking slowed down. Cabrina and Oday looked at each other and smiled.

Brayonna realized that they would be leaving soon, and quickly backed away. She had to get out of there. But which way had she come in? She tried to trace her steps but ended up more lost than before.

She heard them talking, their voices getting closer!

At the door, she fumbled for the pass key that hung around her neck.

They were right around the corner from her!

She slid it over the reader and it beeped loudly. Alarmed, Brayonna opened the door and darted out. She didn't even dare look over her shoulder to see if they saw her.

Quickly, she went back to her desk, but had enough sense to slow down to a casual walk when she was in view of it, and sat down. Her heart was pounding.

"Find what you needed, Brayonna?"

She jumped at the voice. It was Leeda, peeking over the partition down at her, smiling.

"Uh, no," she fumbled for an excuse. What could she tell her: she was to busy spying on her manager and the assistant fucking each others brains out in the back room? "I'll look again later, after lunch."

Leeda nodded. "Yeah, that place is a little confusing at first. But you'll get use to it." Just then she looked up, and her smile turned into a little smirk.

Brayonna followed her gaze, and her breath caught.

Oday and Cabrina were walking together, from the direction of the filing room. They looked like any other pair of coworkers going about their innocent business. To the casual eye, anyway. Brayonna could tell they both looked a little piqued from their physical exertion.

To her relief, neither one looked in her direction, instead they walked past her and Leeda, lost in conversation that certainly was all business. Then they disappeared around the corner, heading to his office.

They hide it well, she thought to herself.

"They don't hide it very well, do they?" said Leeda. It was more of a statement than a question.

Brayonna was shocked, but managed to keep her expression neutral. "Hide what?" she asked, the perfect picture of innocence.

Leeda started, as if realizing she said too much. But after a moment she shrugged. "Oh, hell, you're going to eventually find out anyway. Its not like their little escapades aren't a company secret."

Brayonna still did not reveal what she knew, but asked, "What secret?"

"That they like to fuck in the office, whenever they can."

"What?!" she said, with mock surprise. "No way!"

Leeda nodded and leaned closer, conspiratorially. "Oh, yeah. Everyday, almost. Or so it seems. They've been doing it for as long as I've been here, and I started about two years ago." She shrugged, "No big deal really. Doesn't effect their work, or any of the relationships with their coworkers. So no one says anything."

Brayonna beetle her eyebrows with concern, "Won't they get in trouble if they do get caught?"

Leeda shook her head, "Doubt it. Oday is the prodigal son. His dad owns the company."

"Really?" said Brayonna.

Leeda continued, "In fact, I know for certain that Oday's old man, who started this company decades ago, use to do the same thing. Usually with a lot of the temp workers. Made a point of bringing on all the cute girls he could find and then screw their brains out."

Brayonna's eyes were wide. "Like father, like son, I guess."

Leeda laughed. "True, but it's best not to bring this up with anyone else. Everyone just goes along with it and there aren't any problems. I'd recommend you do the same."

"My lips are sealed," said Brayonna.

She felt a little better now. Accidentally, finding them like that seems to be a regular event around here, anyway. It wasn't like she was the first to have this happen to her. It seemed almost generational.

She and Leeda returned to work, and Brayonna did her best to blank the event from her mind. But over and over, the vision of Cabrina gobbling down Oday's cock played in her mind.

She had wanted it to be her doing that gobbling.

Eventually, she managed to make it through the whole day without anything else happening, at least not rutting coworker related. As it got close to quitting time, she found herself leaping at the sound of another voice over her shoulder.

"Brayonna, could you do me a favour?"

She turned.

It was Cabrina!

She composed herself and said, "Sure, what do you need?"

Cabrina smiled sweetly at her, "Could you reanalyze that marketing report you just sent me? I need to be doubly sure it's accurate. I know it would mean you may have to stay a little late. Would that be okay?"

"Uh, sure. Of course." Brayonna said. What else was she going to say on her first day of work? No? Still, she wondered if this was a ploy for Cabrina to give her hell once everyone was gone. But the other woman's face revealed nothing, and she doubted she had anything to fear.

"Great," said Cabrina. "Could you actually print it out and bring it to me, when its done? I'm afraid I'm all caught in something and might not check my email in time."

Brayonna said she would, and Cabrina went back to her desk.

"Brown noser," teased Leeda, as she put on her coat. "I guess we can't go for those drinks after, huh?"

"Oh, not this time. Maybe tomorrow," Brayonna said.

After Leeda left, Brayonna returned to the marketing report. She was quite certain she hadn't missed anything the first time around, but if it was as important as Cabrina said then she made sure to be even more thorough.

When she finished, she printed it out. At the printer, she stretched feeling her bones pop from having sat for so many hours. She looked around. The office was empty, and it was getting dark outside. How long had she been working? A couple of hours? Everyone else was gone.

She went over to Cabrina's desk. Most of the office lights had been dimmed or turned off in this section, except for a lamp on Cabrina's desk, and a couple more in Oday's office. His door was open, and she could her him talking on the phone.

Cabrina graciously took the report. "Thank you, so much. I really appreciate you making the extra effort. It's something we look for in our workers."

"No problem," said Brayonna, she was ready to leave. Having watched sex that day, made her want some herself. Maybe she would call up an old boyfriend or two and fish for her own private session.

"Will there be anything else?" she asked.

"Actually, now that you mention it, there is. Oday wanted to talk to you briefly before you left for the evening. Do you have time?"

Again, what was she going to say on her first day? No?

"No problem," she said, not really meaning it. She hoped this wouldn't take to long. She had sex to schedule, after all.

"Great," said Cabrina. "Go right in and have a seat. He's on the phone but shouldn't be too much longer."

Brayonna went into the office and saw Oday behind his desk. His eyebrows went up when he noticed her and indicated she should sit down, so she did.

As he finished his conversation, his eyes kept going to Brayonna, and making no effort to hide the fact he was checking her out.

Well, she thought, *this is interesting.*

After a few more moments, he hung up and smiled at her. "Sorry about that," he said. "Work is never done around here."

"I know what you mean," she agreed, not knowing what else to say. Always best to agree with the manager.

"How are things going?"

"Great, thank you."

"Getting along okay? Getting up to speed with the work?"

"You bet. I look forward to more."

He smiled, and paused for a moment, regarding her.

"Actually, I was looking forward to more from you, too." His smile turned into a grin.

Not sure what this meant, Brayonna simply grinned back. "Ah, good," was all she managed to say.

"I have something to show you, if you still have a minute or two. Shouldn't take long."

"Sure, what is it?"

He stood up from his desk and walked around to towards her. He had a remote control in his hands. "Check this out. I think you will find this very interesting."

He pointed it at a large big screen television mounted on the side wall, and turned it on.

Intrigued, Brayonna turned to watch it.

It was a video of a room, and she instantly recognized it as the filing room in the back of the office, with a time code playing at the bottom. She also instantly knew what section the camera was angled on.

Uh oh, she thought, alarm growing.

Into frame walked two people: Oday and Cabrina. For a few moments they kiss, and then things quickly progress to where Oday was screwing Cabrina on the pile of boxes.

Then, from the left of frame, Brayonna saw herself enter, practically tip toeing along, to peer around the filing cabinet at them.

Oday had been watching her reaction. "We always like to watch ourselves afterword," he said. "It's more arousing that way. Sneaking around, and doing it while others are nearby. Its exciting for us."

Brayonna was paralysed, unsure of what she was to say. The on-screen Oday was now finished, and Cabrina was sucking him off. Brayonna remembered wanting to know what that was like with him.

Guess that was outta the question now, just like her job.

"We were surprised you found us so soon. We try to be careful," he said.

There was a noise behind Brayonna and she turned to see Cabrina enter. Her face was somber, but not angry. In fact, Oday didn't seem upset either. *Maybe that was a good thing*, she thought, hopefully.

Cabrina walked over to stand next to Oday, he put his arm around her waist. She said, "We normally delete these right after, just to be safe. But something got our attention."

Both Cabrina and Oday looked back at the screen. Not wanting too, but feeling she had to see this through, she did as well.

As Cabrina finished sucking off Oday, Brayonna saw herself playing with her own breasts. The look on her face was lustful, even emoting a sexual hunger.

She looked very turned on.

Oday stopped the video, and he and Cabrina looked at Brayonna.

Brayonna felt ashamed, and said, "I'm so sorry... it was a mistake. I never intended to intrude on you guys, I was just..." Oday held up a hand to stop her. He was smiling.

"It's cool," he said, and looked like he meant it. Cabrina was smiling as well. "You are not in trouble at all. Your job is not at risk. Life will go on as normal, if you are still willing to stay on with us despite this embarrassing little event."

Brayonna suddenly felt tremendous relief. "Yes! Oh, thank you. I feel some much better now!" She certainly did.

Oday then said, "Well, that's the thing. You may feel better about this, but since you appeared to enjoy what Cabrina and I were doing, we were wondering if we could make you feel a lot more better." He grinned.

Cabrina said, "A whole hell of a lot better."

Brayonna's eyes widened at what they were suggesting.

Cabrina said, "Besides, with three people, I think a whole lot of market research could get done."

"Some great, serious sweaty market research, too," said Oday.

Brayonna found herself smiling along with them. "That's a great idea. I could use some market research, too."

They all chuckled.

Then, Cabrina reached up, undid the buttons on her blouse, slowly revealing her ample cleavage. Brayonna watched, transfixed. Cabrina then pulled her dress down letting it fall to the floor. She then stepped out of it. As she was wearing nothing underneath, Brayonna had a wonderful eyeful. She was quite curvy, with a well defined hourglass figure.

Impulsively, Brayonna stood, and walked over to her. She said, "Wow, impressive."

Cabrina smiled, "I know."

Brayonna reached up and cupped the other woman's large breasts, squeezing and massaging them. They were quite heavy and firm.

The women kissed, mouths open, teething and sucking on each other's lips.

Oday watched them with wide, hungry eyes. He quickly undid the buttons on his shirt, and pulled off his tie. Then he unbuckled his belt, and dropped his pants. His erect penis poked hard against the inside of his boxer shorts.

Not to be left out, Brayonna started to undo her dress, as well. Cabrina giggled and helped her, occasionally trading kisses. When it was loose enough, she yanked it down, suddenly exposing Brayonna's naked body. Her firm ass shook with the motion.

"Looks like neither of us don't believe in wearing underwear," said Brayonna, grinning.

"Maybe you girls can help me with mine?" asked Oday.

The girls went over to him, and got down on their knees side by side, in front of him. Cabrina said to Brayonna, "Be my guest."

Brayonna pulled down Oday's underwear, causing his hard dick to bob and sway. She grabbed it, smiled up at Oday, leaned forward and put it in her mouth. She started to suck.

As she did this, Cabrina ran one hand over her ass exploring its shape, with the other she reached between Brayonna's thighs and started to gently rub at her pussy.

Pleased with the sensation, Oday put his hands on either side of Brayonna's head to guide its movement as she moved it up and down, sucking and slurping.

Brayonna developed a rhythm, making sure she got further down his shaft as she bobbed. One hand was stroking him, and she matched its movements with her mouth. Her other hand was braced on one of his muscular thighs.

Cabrina bent over and started to kiss Brayonna's butt cheeks, occasionally biting. She kept her other hands fingers rubbing at her pussy, which was getting wet. For several minutes they enjoyed each other like this.

Brayonna stopped sucking him off for a moment, and switched her attention to his hanging balls. While continuing to stroke him, she tickled them with her tongue, then she sucked them into her mouth, exploring their contours.

Cabrina leaned over, and took Oday's wet prick into her mouth and flickered her tongue over it while Brayonna stroked it for her. Oday moaned while the two women sucked on his cock on balls.

Then Brayonna said, "I have an idea." She stood, and pulling Oday by his dick, went to the desk. Cabrina followed, smiling.

Brayonna pushed aside some papers and pens which fell on the floor. Then, she slide up on to the desk, leaned back and spread her legs wide.

"You two have some work to do," she said. She slapped at her pussy with one hand and offered a grin.

The others obliged.

Oday went over to Brayonna, bent down and gave her pussy a few long licks. Cabrina went around to the other side of the desk, cupped one of Brayonna's breasts and and latched onto its nipple with her mouth, sucking loudly.

Then, Oday took his dick and slapped it against Brayonna's clit, and her inner thighs. Brayonna rubbed his flat stomach, enjoying the feel of his abs.

He then used his prick to rub against her pussy lips, moving them about, helping them open a little. He could see she was now very wet. Then he stuck it in, and slowly eased his length into her.

Brayonna groaned, and lay flat on her back, knocking more papers to the floor. Cabrina rubbed both her own clit, and Brayonna's, feeling Oday's dick slide between her exploring fingers.

Then Cabrina placed one of her breasts over Brayonna's mouth, its size nearly smothering her face. As Brayonna kissed and sucked on it, she took one of Brayonna's breasts in her own mouth, biting gently, and licking at the nipple.

Oday began thrusting into Brayonna, holding her legs up. Faster and faster he fucked her as the girls played with each other's tits. Again and again he pounded against her.

Then, he pulled out of her, guided her off the desk and turned her around to bend her over it. Her ass was magnificent, and he smacked at it, watching the firmness of her flesh move. Then he slide is cock into her.

As he did this, Cabrina crawled up onto the desk and positioned herself so her pussy was now in Brayonna's face. Brayonna gladly took the offering, and began to lick at her wet pussy. Oday pounded her from behind.

Cabrina played with her own tits, pulling them one at a time up to her mouth and sucking on the nipples, squeezing them. She watched eagerly as Oday fucked Brayonna, enjoying the view from her position.

Brayonna flicked Cabrina's clit with her tongue, then gave her pussy long sensual licks. As Oday continued to smack against her ass, she latched onto Cabrina's clit and sucked it up between her teeth. She flicked it with her tongue.

For several long, wonderful minutes they worked on each other like this and the office filled with the sounds of their passion: slurping, sucking, licking, smacking of flesh on flesh.

Oday had a firm grasp of Brayonna's ass, and he pounded it harder and harder, almost like a machine.

Cabrina let Brayonna eat her pussy out for a while longer, then she said, "My turn to taste you."

So they switched positions. While the girls manoeuvred, Oday slipped out of Brayonna and stroked his dick, keeping it hard.

Brayonna, again sat on the desk, leaning back, while Cabrina bent in front of Oday. He slipped inside her, enjoying the shape of her ass. Cabrina began to lick at Brayonna's pussy which was raw from being pounded so hard.

They fucked like this for a long time, sweat beading on their skin. The office was getting warm from their combined body heat.

Eventually, Oday couldn't handle any more, and said, "I'm going to pop!"

Quickly, he withdrew from Cabrina and stood back, stroking his cock. The two women went to their knees, positioning themselves in front of him, looking up with eager eyes. They placed an arm around each other's waist, breasts touching.

Furiously stroking his dick, Oday moaned loudly. Hot cum squirt out of him, spraying the sweaty women, who laughed with delight. White sticky strands splattered over their flesh; their breasts and their faces.

When he was done, Oday sagged, but not before Brayonna grabbed his dick and sucked on it, getting every little bit of his cum out of it. Cabrina leaned over and lapped at Brayonna's tits, which were covered in cum, hungrily sucking up what she could.

Finished with Oday, Brayonna grabbed Cabrina's head and positioned her underneath her. Cabrina opened her mouth wide, looking up at her.

Brayonna slowly spit out long strands of cum onto the other woman's tongue, watching it slide down and pool at the back of her throat. When there was no more to receive, Cabrina swallowed.

Brayonna licked Cabrina's tits clean, until they glowed with her spit.

Gasping for air they all looked to one another and laughed.

Brayonna smiled at them both, fully satisfied, and said, “Glad I came for that interview!”

END

The Roommate

That morning, Lucinda woke to find herself in one of her moods: hot, bothered, and craving for a little trouble.

"Today, I think I'm gonna get me some," she declared with triumph.

Intent on doing something about it, she called in sick to work. As a reporter for a foreign affairs web site, she knew skipping out for even a day would cost her later on. But, today, she just wanted to experience some of the things she had written about first hand. Why should famous people be the only ones allowed to have all the kinky fun?

Having never played hooky before, she found making an impulsive decision like this exhilarating.

Her cell warbled, and her heart leaped into her throat. Was work checking on her fib *already*?

She picked it up and looked at the call display. She laughed. No, it was Akeely, her best friend in the whole world. Lucinda knew Akeely had quite the adventurous side. Maybe she should find out just how adventurous it could be?

"Hey, Akeely! Why the early morning call?" she said. "Checking to see if I'm up to some mischief?" She wasn't at the moment, but that was going to change.

"Lucinda, baby," Akeely said, sounding despondent. "I wish it were true." Her normally giddy personality was no where to be found this morning.

"What happened?"

"How, it's shitty. Asher's been cheating on me!"

"Oh, my God!" Lucinda cried out. "What a bastard! What happened?" As she said this Lucinda was shocked to realize she had slipped her free hand down the front of her pink panties.

Delightfully moist flesh welcomed her fingers.

Akeely had started to cry. "I was cleaning out the front closet, getting ready to move some of the winter wear out of the way. Anyways, I was about to do the same to that big, puffy, blue jacket Asher wears and checked the pockets first."

She stopped and sniffled loudly.

"Go on," said Lucinda. She was slowly rubbing her middle and fore fingers up and down the length of her pussy, enjoying the hot dampness that was spreading down there. She tried to suppress a shudder by biting a corner of her bottom lip.

Akeely, oblivious, said, "I found a box of condoms in the inside pocket."

"So?"

"So?!" Akeely yelled. "We've been on the pill for months. But what makes it even worse was the box was half empty!"

"What an asshole," Lucinda gasped. Her fingers were now moving more vigorously. What had come over her? Was it Akeely's voice that was turning her on, or the fact that her friend was now technically *single*?

"Are you okay?" Akeely asked. "Did I catch you at a bad time, or something?" Her voice had pitched higher with annoyance.

"No! Not at all!" said Lucinda. "Oh, I'm sorry sweetie. This is just so much to take in all of a sudden." And with that she firmly thrust a finger deep inside herself. She was very hot and slick, just the way she liked it. It took all her effort not to moan out load.

She as being so naughty! Perhaps it had to do with her long dry spell from intimacy. It had been months since she felt the flesh of another person's body on her.

Or in her.

She tried to at least sound consoling. "Have you confronted him, yet?" Rub, rub, rub.

"I sent him a text a few minutes ago. Just said FOUND YOUR RUBBERS, and left it at that. Haven't heard anything back."

"Well, he probably hasn't seen it yet. Does he work on site today?" Asher was a construction supervisor, and his work in the field resulted in him missing phone calls and texts.

"Yeah, I think so. Oh, what do I do now, Lucinda? I'm afraid of how he'll react!"

Lucinda had moved her hand up to her mouth, sniffing experimentally. She put a damp finger into her mouth and sucked. She tasted pretty damn good!

She managed to say, "Who cares now! Don't do anything else, especially when he responds. Let the cheating bastard sweat!"

This didn't really make Akeely feel any better, and she started to sob. "Oh, this is horrible. I trusted him with all my heart! Now what am I going to do? I feel awful."

Lucinda knew exactly how to comfort her friend and make her feel amazingly better at the same time. Besides, she wanted to hear what Akeely thought about her taste, too.

"Akeely, honey, I want you to come over here right away. We can talk about this further. I don't want you to be all by yourself today."

"Oh, that's so kind. But don't you have work to go to?"

Lucinda had licked her finger, and slid it down the the crack of her butt, between her big, rounded cheeks. She started to rub herself down there. It tingled at the touch. Can't leave that part of her outta the fun now, could she?

"No worries, I already called in sick. Wanted to do something more constructive with my day, may as well have that be you." Akeely had no clue how constructive that would be!

"What about that hunky new room mate of yours?"

"He's kicking around here somewhere," Lucinda said. Now there's a thought!

"Well all right. I need to get my mind off this and I think your company will help. Give me a few minutes to wash up and I'll be over soon as I can."

Lucinda was ecstatic. She had now slowly worked her finger. She kept it there, thrusting it in and out with small movements.

She said, "Great! Don't worry we'll work through this together. After all, what are friends for?"

She hung up, and squealed with joy. This was amazing. She had always fantasized about Akeely, and now she had a chance to put those fantasies into action, with the added incentive of making her best friend feel good during a time of need.

No, not just good. *Fantastic!*

She removed her finger and smelled it. There was something strangely arousing about doing something so forbidden. Unsure with what to do with herself until Akeely arrived she went to the big oak dresser and opened the bottom drawer. Inside was a myriad of exotic toys; Dildos, a vibrator, lubricant and a curl of silk rope.

She grabbed a handful of supplies, and jumped up on the bed, kicking away the covers. Won't be needing those.

Laying down, head comfortably propped up on a pillow so she could watch what she was doing, she spread her legs. She took a squeeze bottle of body oil and squirted some in her hand. It felt warm and silky.

At the foot of the bed, mounted on the wall, was a large mirror which she had positioned there for a reason. She had entertained herself with it many times, either by herself, or with company. (And with company was always the most thrilling!)

She watched herself now, from a wonderfully delicious angle. Then, with slow purpose, she began to smear the oil onto her body. Up and down her flat tummy, along the inside of her firm thighs, but staying away from her pussy.

At least for now!

Her breasts were full and perky, and she made sure to rub them over completely. She squeezed them together, enjoying the feel of them. She pinched each nipple and was thrilled at getting them so erect. Leaning forward she took the left one in her mouth, and licked it over playfully. Then she did the same with the right, this time sucking in as much of her own breast into her mouth as she could, flicking the nipple repeatedly with her tongue.

She let it out, with a audible pop, smiling at the beautiful red ring on her flesh it created.

Getting more excited she took the vibrator with one hand, and used her other to rub her pussy. She had a waxing job done earlier in the week and she loved the feel of her bare skin. Wiggling her fingers back and forth, enjoying the wet sound her pussy created, she turned on the vibrator.

She ran the vibrator over her chest and breasts, feeling its mechanical sensation, and ran it around each nipple. Then she guided it slowly down her flat stomach, past her belly button (she had an inny!), and through the small trim triangle of pubic hair.

As it crested her pubic bone she shuddered with anticipation.

Then her cell phone rang.

Dropping the vibrator in alarm, she was suddenly awash with a feeling of guilt. The ringing brought her back into reality. This time, the display showed it was work.

"Uh, oh," she said. Should she answer? If she didn't they might get suspicious. If she was really sick she should be home, by the phone. But if she didn't answer now, they would probably call back later, and that's when she was planning on entertaining Akeely. All of Akeely.

Best to deal with them now. She answered it.

Lucinda! You're alive." It was Dwayne, her boss. "How are you feeling? Lucinda told me you had called in sick and thought I should check in on you, and see how you were doing."

"I'm not feeling to great, Dwayne," she said. He was checking in on her, alright. But not with genuine concern. She made a pathetic attempt at sounding ill. "I hope it's only a 24 hour thing. I'd like to get back to work as we both know the work won't do itself." As opposed to her doing *herself.*

"Yeah, of course. Of course," he said. "Hey, what's that sound? Is that some sort of interference?"

Lucinda balked. It was the vibrator! It was making its high pitched sound. She fumbled for it, but the oil on her hands made it slip out.

"Oh, that's nothing. Just the TV," she managed to grab it and flick it off. She couldn't help but feel a little disappointed.

"Look, if you need anything. Anything at all to help you feel better, just let me know. I can be over in a flash." He sounded like he was grinning from ear to ear.

Lucinda shuddered. Dwayne was short, fat, bald, and always smelled like potatoes. And, yet, that didn't stop him from shamelessly hitting on her, and every other female in the office. He had even groped her on several occasions; at the Christmas party, the Halloween party, the Thanksgiving party. Heck, anytime there was a party he'd guzzle enough alcohol to work up the courage to fondle the local help. He revolted her on so many levels.

He was *definitely* not what she had in mind for today. Or ever for that matter.

But she was smart enough not to let him know that as she said: "Thanks, Dwayne. That's so sweet of you, but I should be able to manage." He was her boss after all, so she had to remain diplomatic, even though he made her skin crawl.

"Okay," Dwayne said, sounding a little disappointed. "Well, if you need anything, just let me know." He hung up.

What she needed could not be provided by him, she thought to herself.

With the moment of passion momentarily lost, she jumped out of bed. She stood before the mirror and admired herself. Her bum stuck out just enough to be appealing, and she knew she looked great in a pair of tight jeans.

She couldn't wait until Akeely saw it for herself. Maybe Lucinda would rub it in her friend's face for a while. They would both most certainly like that!

She smiled to herself. Boy, was Akeely going to have fun today. Lucinda was to do everything in her power to make her best friend forget about her troubles.

There was a banging noise outside her bedroom window. Curious, she tip toed toward it and peaked through the closed curtains. Down below, in the yard was her room mate, Terence. He was busy hammering a piece of wood fixing the sundeck, which had seen one too many parties in its time.

Lucinda's body stiffened, and her eyes widened in admiration.

His shirt was off, and his dark muscular frame was covered in a sheen of sweat. Well formed muscles rippled in the morning sun. He had a grim look of determination on his face, making him look all the more manly. Lucinda was intrigued, and again found her fingers where they didn't belong. Watching him work from up here got her going again.

Now *this* hunk completely eclipsed her pudgy little perverted boss.

"Well, well, well," she said. "Looks like Mister Room Mate is working off some rent."

Perhaps there was a way to kill some time before Akeely's arrival, after all.

She practically skipped downstairs, through the kitchen and into the adjacent dining room. Its sliding glass door, was directly across from where Terence was working. The blinds were open and her skin prickled with anticipation.

Slowly she padded across the linoleum tiles, her feet tingling with their coolness.

She manoeuvred herself around the dining room table and stood completely exposed at the glass. She posed seductively, hands on her hips. But Terence continued to work unaware of the naked beauty only ten, or so, feet away from him. The concentration on his work aroused her even more as she imagined him concentrating on her with the same intensity. Especially with those muscular hands.

Moments passed and still he did not look up. She started to feel foolish and giggled to herself. This was ridiculous. So, with determination, she rapped loudly on the glass.

Still nothing. But after another bout of knocking, Terence looked up.

She took this moment to smile brightly, and pose; hands upraised in a 'ta-da' like manner, almost as if she just jumped out of a big ol'birthday cake.

The reaction was almost instantaneous: Terence dropped his jaw, as well as his hammer. Eyes wide, he stood dumbfounded. She couldn't blame him. This was not quite what you expect to see while working on a patio in your own backyard!

She winked at him, then did a little seductive cat walk, parading back-and-forth to the sides of the glass.

He gawked, and allow himself to smile. She was elated. Progress! Now that she put out the hook, she just had to reel this studly fish in.

She turned around, and arched her back so her curvy rump was prominently displayed. Then, bracing her hands on the edge of the dining room table, she pressed her ass up against the pane, which felt cool on her exposed flesh and bare pussy.

She wiggled playfully.

Glancing over her shoulder, she couldn't help but giggle. Apparently, it was like waving a red flag in front of a bull.

Terence hurried over while still to keeping his hungry eyes locked on her lovely form. She laughed as he slipped and almost fell over. Thankfully, he didn't. She didn't want him injured before the fun could begin.

He stood looking sheepish, perhaps unsure of what was really going on. She could tell from here that she had the desired effect on him. She curled a finger at him, in a come hither manner.

He obeyed, and crossed the short distance with a determined stride.

Standing before her on the other side of the glass she could see he was panting heavily. Sweat glazed his dark bare flesh, accentuating his muscles. She took a moment to appraise him and he indulged her. When she had worked her gaze up his body their eyes finally locked. She could see the hunger in his gaze and she felt the same way.

Something *great* was about to happen.

She leaned forward, ample breasts swaying with the motion, and unlocked the door with a flourishing flick of a finger.

He opened the door and stepped inside, closing it behind him. All the while never taking his gaze off her. She backed up against the dining room table and gave him a coy expression.

She had always been attracted to Terence but, up until now, neither he nor she had done anything about it. Well, that was about to change in a big way.

"Lucinda," Terence said, a little out of breath, eyes all over her. "Uh, what's up?"

"I saw you working out there," she said. She hopped up on the table with a little jump, leaned back and slowly spread her legs wide. "I thought I'd give you something else to hammer for a while. Think you have the tool for the job, Mr. Room Mate?"

She believe he did. His muscular shoulders rose with his deep breathing. He stepped forward. With his callused hands he embraced her slender arms. She could smell the sweat of him and she shuddered in anticipation.

They kissed passionately, his tongue eagerly seeking hers. His strong hands caressed her; her thighs, her back, her bottom and finally her breasts. Squeezing them he pressed his bulging jeans against the wetness between her legs. He was most certainly happy to be there!

He bent down and took a erect nipple in his mouth, sucking and teething it gently. She moaned, and with her hands at the back of his head, pressed him closer. He obliged and switched to the other breast, which ached against his hot mouth.

She played with herself vigorously, and now wanted much more. Pushing him upwards she made him wait as she slowly undid the button of his jeans. Then, as she stuck out a tongue with playful concentration, she unzipped his fly.

With several firm tugs, she managed to pull down his pants revealing his excitement.

"Yummy," she declared. She grabbed his swollen shaft and hungrily took his fat prick into her mouth. She began to work it with a technique that was all her own. He groaned. She managed a smile despite the fat cock impeding the expression.

She sucked on him diligently, stroking up and down, all the while never losing him from her lips. Wet sucking noises filled the empty house, punctuated with the occasional moan from the both of them.

When she was certain he was close to climaxing she eased up just enough to keep the inevitable from happening. She wasn't done with them yet!

"You're not getting off that easy," she said. "Pun intended," she winked at him.

He managed to laugh, and his breathing slowed. She knew she had him under control. This was going better than she had hoped.

"Let's get creative," she said, and pushed him back a little while dropping to her knees. He grinned down at her like a horny teenager.

"Not what you think, big guy," she offered an evil grin. "Turn around."

He didn't move right away, momentarily confused as to her intent. She arched a brow and said, "Aren't you curious as to how freaky I can get?"

His eyes widened but he did as he was told.

She giggled and smacked his hairy bum. His muscular buttocks were incredibly firm and resembled the two halves of basketball.

"God, I'm a lucky girl!" She took a butt cheek in each hand and spread them as far as they would go, exposing his asshole. "And you, Mister Roommate, are a very, very lucky boy."

And with that declaration she shoved her face fully into his ass. He moaned loudly.

Slowly, she worked her wet, hot tongue slowly over his ass-hole, again and again. The feel of his flesh against her cheeks, and even her ears, excited her tremendously.

After a few minutes of intense and licking, and exaggerated slurping sounds for effect, she reached around him with both hands and stroked his cock. One hand gripping his length, while using the thumb of the other to rub the tip of its engorged head.

Then, with well practised technique and bold determination, she slowly worked the tip of her tongue inside him, all the while keeping his ass-hole encompassed by her hungry lips.

With careful management, she kept him from exploding even though it felt like you could pop at any moment.

She felt the sweat from his back trickle down his back, roll down his butt, and over her nose, which was firmly planted against his tail bone. She managed a muffled chuckle as she thrust her tongue deeper, keeping his hot flesh pressed against her.

"Jesus, you are a dirty girl," he was able to say between excited breaths. She wanted to give a playful response but she was too busy.

They continued like this for several minutes. She eventually took one hand away and slid it between his muscular thighs, and grabbed his balls firmly. She kneading them gently.

He shuddered and shook with the intensity of their act.

When she was satisfied she had worked enough wonders, she put both her arms underneath him. Then she guided him backwards until he was above her, until he was practically straddling her up-turned face. As he leaned against the dining room table for balance, she took his balls in her mouth.

Again, she sucked, sometimes popping them out with a flourish, only to immediately take them back in again. She used her probing tongue to explore their form and move them around her mouth playfully. All the while she had a magnificent view of his ass, with her nose jammed up in it. He reached down and squeezed her tits, occasionally pinching their erect nipples.

He trembled, and she moaned with the satisfaction that she had him right where she wanted him.

This was her way of doing things, working one part of the body for as long as was possible until the recipient was close to complete Nirvana. If anything, she was a trooper.

Because of her greedy slurping, and load moaning, she didn't notice he was trying to say something until he reached back to place a palm on her forehead, indicating she should stop. Disappointed, she let his balls go with a wet pop of her lips. The dangled, glistening with her spit.

"What?" she asked while getting a good gasp of air.

"Someone is at the front door!" he exclaimed. Worry edged his voice.

Then she heard it. The doorbell!

"Oh, my God," she said. "It's Akeely!"

How could she have forgotten about her so soon? Of course, seeing Terence's naked form before her, she knew very well why.

She jumped up. "Wait here," she commanded, and giggled at his uncertainty as she left the dining room.

"Akeely?" he called after her. "Your friend?"

She ran through the house. Every inch of her skin tingled with the excitement of this sexual adventure, and heart pounded as fast as a bird's.

When she reached the door she peered through the peep hole. Akeely was outside, looking distraught.

Taking a deep breath to calm her nerves she opened the door, but shielded her nakedness with it. She stuck her head out and said, "Akeely, baby! Get in here!"

Akeely was still very upset, and marched inside without even looking at her. "I'm a nervous wreck, and nearly got into two accidents on the way over. I swear I hit every red light in the city. I tell you I'm in need of very good distraction from my problems right now..."

Her voice trailed off as she turned and saw Lucinda's naked body, which gleamed with sweat and oil. For a moment she said nothing and just gawked.

Unsure as to what to do Lucinda did her 'ta-da' pose.

"Lucinda!" Akeely managed. To say she looked surprised was an understatement in the extreme.

"Akeely!" Lucinda returned.

"You're.... you're buck naked!"

"And you are not," Lucinda said, putting her hands on her hips and giving the best pouting expression she could muster.

"What do we do about this? We can't have such a disparaging difference in my house, now can we?"

"Uh..." was all Akeely could say. Despite her surprise Akeely's eyes continually moved over her body. Taking in each part one by one, only to repeat the cycle again. Lucinda suspected she was impressed, and perhaps more than a little smitten with the view.

Lucinda smiled. "I am spectacular, aren't I?"

Akeely's mouth moved but words didn't come out at first. After a few moments of trying, and with eyes still roving, she finally asked, "What's going on?"

Lucinda frowned a little, and moved forward until she was standing almost nose to nose with her. She took in Akeely's face with her gaze; her lips, her cheeks, her forehand, her little pug nose, and finally settled on her big brown eyes. "What's going on is I'm going to help you forget about all your problems for the next little while. This is something I've been wanting to do to you... *with you*, for a very long time."

As she finished speaking she placed her arms around Akeely's waist.

"I... I don't know..." but Akeely couldn't finish because Lucinda suddenly kissed her and deeply. They remain locked like that for several long tense moments. Then Lucinda felt Akeely's body slowly become less rigid and finally press against her own.

She was pleased when she realized Akeely was returning the kiss just as passionately as she was giving it.

Their tongues rolled playfully around, taking turns flicking in and out of each others mouth. Hot kissing turned to soft moans.

They used their hands to explore the others body, pressing and rubbing, with a lot of creative groping thrown in for good measure. Before Lucinda even realized it, she had her best friend up against the wall. One hand deftly plucked the buttons open on Akeely's blouse just enough to thrust a hand inside, and clasp a cup of her ample bra. The other hand surreptitiously slipped its way down the inside of Akeely's skirt, pressing against the hot flush of her belly, and past the welcome thatch of her pubic hair.

With gentle firmness, and perhaps with more than a little expertise, Lucinda slid her fingers over Akeely's pussy. Akeely had grabbed Lucinda's ass, and pressed her against herself as a welcoming gesture.

They both groaned into the others mouth.

Caught up in the passion and heat of the moment they both began to furiously grind against each other. Eventually, between kissing, groping and giggling, they managed to remove all of Akeely's clothes.

For a moment they stopped and held each other at arms length, taking each other in. Akeely's eyes were bright with excitement. "Good, God, you are one sexy bitch!" she said.

Lucinda laughed, "And don't I know it. But you..." she said, while slowly pushing her across the living room and down into a sitting position on the couch. "You are just damn lick-able."

She eased Akeely back. Lucinda pushed Akeely's knees back, exposing not only a luscious round rump, but a beautiful pussy, and a very tasty looking ass-hole. Lucinda gave both an appraising sniff.

"Mmmmm," she said, like someone about to partake of a wonderful desert. "And I know just where to start."

Lucinda then playfully licked the little ass-hole a few times, causing Akeely to yelp in surprise. Lucinda grinned, massaging it slowly with her wet tongue, rotating over and over until Akeely was quivering in ecstasy.

While she worked, Lucinda reached out and gently cupped each of Akeely's pert breasts. They were large, and perfectly formed, and jiggled in her grasp.

With her tongue working every contour, Lucinda could not help but notice the wonderful smell of the pussy pressed against her nose. Akeely massaged her own clit, and the wet sound it made drove them both insane.

Suddenly, Akeely gasped as her eyes went wide. But not with the excitement of the moment. Lucinda stopped and turned to see what she was looking at.

Terence stood in the doorway of the kitchen, naked. His cock was large, and very erect. How could anyone blame him considering what he had been watching.

"Oh, my God! Terence?" Akeely asked, her eyes firmly locked on Terence's big dick.

"He's turned out to be a great room mate. He was helping me with something earlier, and doing a fine job of it, too." She looked over her shoulder at Terence. "Maybe we can just pick up where we left off, huh?"

Terence was practically salivating at this point and didn't require any further coaxing. He quickly walked across the room and got on his knees behind Lucinda. He took a moment to run his hands over her ass, smacking it several times causing her to giggle. The movement of her flesh excited him even more.

He licked one of his thumbs, getting it nice and wet. He then rubbed it around her welcoming ass-hole.

While Terence explored her, Lucinda turned her attention to Akeely's neglected pussy. Akeely watched with wide eyes, mouth open in anticipation.

"I've been wanting to taste you for a very long time," Lucinda said, looking up at her. Then, she gave her a nice long lick; starting from the bottom of Akeely's ass-hole, then slowly up her taint, and then along the length of her wet pussy. She ended at the clitoris, which she then sucked in between her lips. Firmly latched on, she tickled it with the tip of her tongue.

Akeely groaned, reaching down and managed to cup Lucinda's tits with her hands. She squeezed them over and over, feeling their hardened nipples in her palms.

Terence took his hard cock and bounced it playfully off Lucinda's ass several times. He watched as her buttocks jiggled. Then he guided it down, and very slowly slipped the tip of it into her waiting pussy. He was glad to find she was soaking wet down there, and slid it in further. Lucinda paused in her vigorous licking to gasp with the penetration, but quickly resumed her work.

They went at it like this for several long, wondrous minutes, and time vanished in a passionate blur. Terence pounding her from behind, while squeezing her ass. Lucinda licking, and sometimes pressing her face into Akeely's pussy, shaking it quickly from side to side while sucking harder. Akeely did her best to stay conscious, while squeezing Lucinda's tits, and sometimes her own.

Terence then took control, pulling himself out of Lucinda. He got her to stand up, and then he guided her forward onto

Akeely, so she was now straddling Akeely's face. Akeely indulged them by grabbing Lucinda's ass and pulling her closer so her pussy was now in her face. Lucinda used the top of the couch for balance, while looking down past her own jiggling breasts at Akeely's eyes, which looked up at her. The tip of Akeely's nose poked up through Lucinda's pubic hair.

Akeely's mouth worked wonders, sucking and licking with enthusiasm. Lucinda gyrated her hips back and forth and loved the feel Akeely's nose rub against her clit, and occasionally inside her.

Not to miss out on the fun, Terence hovered between Akeely's widely outstretched legs and suddenly jammed his cock down deep inside her waiting pussy. They both grunted with the roughness of the motion. Then, bracing arms on the couch where he could, he began moving his hips up and down. He pulled himself out almost the full length of his dick, until it nearly unsheathed itself, and then slamming it back down with pleasurable force. Over and over he did this, while his face was pressed up against Lucinda's gyrating ass, which he kissed and bit.

The house filled with the noise of their mutual love making; the near ceaseless smacking of flesh on flesh, the hungry slurping and sucking, groans, moans, the occasion incomprehensible word indicating pleasure.

Long minutes passed, until, without a word of discussion, they switched positions. This time, Terence lay on the carpeted floor, his muscular body outstretched. He smiled up at the girls. "Have a seat ladies," he said.

Akeely gave Lucinda's pussy a final sucking lick, and Lucinda smacked her ass as a reward.

Lucinda made a show of trying to pick where on Terence's body she wanted to try, then settled for his dick. She squatted over him, throwing a leg over his waist. She grabbed his manhood, and pointed it up at her. She used his prick to caress her pussy lips, teasingly.

"You want this?" she whispered. Terence nodded. Lucinda grinned evilly, "You sure?"

Akeely then leaned onto Terence's chest, swung her ass over his face, and pushed back, sitting on him. His mouth and nose were now buried in her. He grunted and licked.

"I think he wants this, too," Akeely said.

Lucinda suddenly jammed down onto Terence, forcing his cock all the way insider her. Using her the taught muscles of her legs, she moved up and down the length of him, balancing on the abs of his stomach with her hands. The quick motions, and having him deep insider her, nearly brought her to climax. Akeely rubbed her pussy and ass all over Terence's face, causing him to sometimes have trouble breathing. He did not complain in the least.

She leaned forward and kissed Akeely, their mouths wide, tongues diving deeper. They played with each others tits, squeezing, pinching and occasionally smacking them. They took turns suckling each others nipples, tickling the tip of each with their tongues, while casting big eyes ups up at the others face.

Soon, both girls started to made an effort to out grind the other, harder and harder. Faster and faster. Terence groaned, and even hissed with the effort of trying not to explode too soon. His face was now completely glazed with Akeely's wetness, and some even dribbled down through the stubble of his chin to make a tiny pool in the hollow of his throat.

Eventually the intensity caught up to him, and Terence managed to moan from inside Akeely's wet pussy, "I'm gonna cum!"

Quickly, the girls hopped off, and Terence then stood stroking, his shaft. Lucinda dropped down onto her knees before him. Akeely joined her and they both looked up smiling expectantly.

"Yeah, alright," said Lucinda. "Feeding time! I'm hungry!

Akeely pouted, a little. "Give me some, too!" She licked her lips for emphasis.

Knowing what they were waiting for he kept stroking himself while taking turns shoving his fat prick into Lucinda's mouth, and then Akeely's. They both sucked at it until the spit dribbled from their chins. Lucinda even took as much of his length in as possible, causing her to gag when his cock jammed the back of her throat.

Hungry with anticipation, the girls fingered one another.

Finally, Terence let out a gasp, and squirt his pent-up load with a tremendous moan. He made sure both girls got an equal share, glazing their faces. They laughed as they each tried to get more. When there was nothing left to spray he collapsed to the floor in exhaustion.

Lucinda and Akeely then licked each others faces, getting as much of the hot cum as they could. They then kissed passionately, exchanging their share of his seed back and forth.

Lucinda finally sucked on Akeely's chin, careful to get everything that was hanging there. Then she swallowed loudly.

Akeely took a moment to slurp up what was left on Lucinda's face, and swallowed as well.

The girls laughed at their naughtiness, and joined Terence on the floor, one on each side of him. For several long minutes they just breathed heavily, and wallowed in each others sweaty glow.

"Wow," said Akeely. "That was incredible!"

"Wow," said Terence. "That was amazing!"

"Wow," said Lucinda. "That was fantastic!"

They gave each other a tired, but enthusiastic, high-five.

They all laughed.

Lucinda looked over at Akeely, "Oh, Akeely, baby, I have all these wonderful toys in the bedroom I wanted to use on you!"

Akeely grinned. "I'm not going anywhere. I have the whole day to spend here. You were right, earlier, when you said you could distract me from my problems. Why on Earth would I want to leave?"

Terence chuckled. "My patio can wait until next summer, at this rate!"

Again, they laughed.

And with a smile to them both, Lucinda used her hands to pull them over her. She pushed at the back of their heads, guiding their mouths; one for each nipple. They both sucked, and teethed, with gusto, exchanging glances at each other across Lucinda's heaving bosom.

One of them (she couldn't see which, and it certainly didn't matter, anymore) caressed her raw, and incredibly sensitive, clit.

Lucinda arched her back and moaned. It was at this moment she reached a thunderous realization:

She needed to call in sick more often!
END.

www.ingramcontent.com/pod-product-compliance
Ingram Content Group UK Ltd.
Pitfield, Milton Keynes, MK11 3LW, UK
UKHW021936190726
13853UKWH00004B/1479